The Legend and the Lie

By Michael Watermeyer

Published by Michael Watermeyer, United Kingdom.

Author: Michael Watermeyer
Cover design: Michael Watermeyer
Editor: Rosanne Catalano

Cover composition original source images used under
license from Shutterstock.com.
Image of girl's body: copyright © 2017, Tom Volkov/Shutterstock.com.
Image of girl's head: copyright © 2019, Agnieszka Marcinska/Shutterstock.com.
Image of forest: copyright © 2017, Elena Schweitzer/Shutterstock.com.

Image of boy's head: © Oliver Ragfelt/Unsplash.com.
Image of palace: copyright © 2017, Michael Watermeyer.

ISBN: 978-0-9928678-1-2

To Elijah, strong and wise,
and Anna-Sophia, brave and true.

Contents

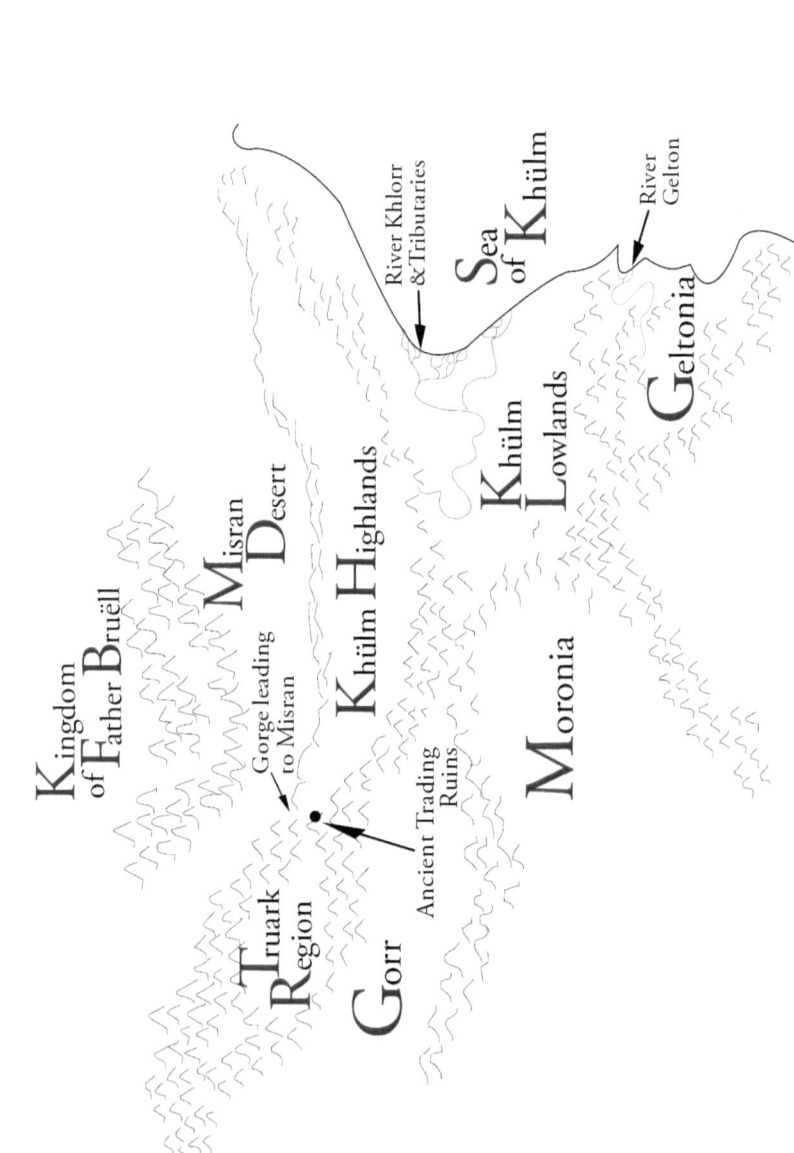

Kingdom
of Father Bruëll

Misran Desert

Khülm Highlands

Khülm Lowlands

Moronia

Gorr

Truark Region

Ancient Trading Ruins

Gorge leading to Misran

River Khlorr & Tributaries

Sea of Khülm

River Gelton

Geltonia

Chapter One

Dusty Roads to Nowhere

Lub-dub.
Lub-dub.
Lub-dub.

I could hear only the sound of my heart pounding in my ears. The noises of the forest, from the chattering night birds to a hooting owl, all faded away. Terrified, I pushed on out of curiosity, one step at a time. I stepped slower and slower, until I stood at the very edge of the river. I froze, too afraid to look, but too riveted to leave. A young boy at the time, no more than twelve, I didn't know my life was about to change forever.

I'm getting ahead of myself. Let's go back to where it all started, and I'll introduce you to Aunt Anne.

Anne was my dad's oldest sister, and what a person she was. She lived a peculiar life, with strong black coffee, weird paintings, and chaos as her constant companions.

One morning, out of the blue, she announced that she would be moving to South Africa. Apparently, she had bought a farm in the middle of a wilderness. No one knew what she thought she was doing; she certainly had no idea about farming. We lived in Spain at the time, mainly because of Dad's work, and South Africa seemed a million miles away. Nevertheless, that December, we became the first family members to visit her—it was all Dad's idea!

I'll never forget the first day we arrived.

Bump.
Creak.

Rattle.

Bump.

After the eleven-hour flight from Spain, I had to survive an endless drive in the backseat of our hired car. I was hot, sweaty, tired, and irritable. To make matters worse, the engine began to overheat as we climbed the final hill on a long, dusty road. In the four hours since we had turned off the highway, it had been nothing but vague directions and endless farm gates.

"This stinks!" I exclaimed under my breath. "Why didn't Aunt Anne buy a farm somewhere closer?"

Did we *have* to finish the whole trip without stopping? Not really—but Mum and Dad wanted to tough it out and get it done as quickly as possible. I looked out of the window and tried to forget the whole thing.

Before us, a huge, dry valley opened towards the setting sun. In the distance, a lazy river meandered its way between clumps of willow trees, irrigated fields, and thickets of bull rushes. Although the high, winding road gave us a wonderful view, the sheer cliff falling away to one side made me nervous. Dad picked his way down the narrow gravel road, completely absorbed, determined to complete the journey. The lighthearted tune he had whistled in the morning had changed to irritable muttering by now.

My thoughts wandered. What would this trip be like? Would Aunt Anne remember me? She never did. For starters, she usually called me Luke. Worse than that, she thought that I didn't like sweets, which really annoyed me. What were the possibilities? Three weeks of imprisonment with a strange aunt and irritable parents, or a real adventure packed with exploration, new friends, late nights, and early mornings? I sank back into my seat. Either way, I had no idea what lay ahead; I wasn't too sure I liked that very much.

Bump.

Rattle.

Bump.

Rattle.

As we continued down into the valley, the sun dropped further and further below the horizon, splashing out gentle washes of red and orange as it slid away. Dad turned on the headlights, hunched right up to the steering wheel, and squinted through his glasses at the fading image of the road ahead. We eventually ended up on a gentle winding lane that followed the banks of the river through open farmlands. Here and there, a small hare would bounce across our path and disappear into the undergrowth. The endless ringing of cicadas started up, filling the air with a loud chorus. I rolled down the window and stuck my head out, taking in a deep, long breath of the fresh air, full of rich, earthy smells.

"Yes," I said quietly to myself, "I can have adventures here."

All of a sudden we stopped. Dad grunted and Mum pulled out a piece of paper. She peered at it, shook her head, and passed it over to Dad. He squinted at the crumpled little note and then reversed about fifty yards back down the lane. There, beside an enormous tree, stood a rusted old gate. I hopped out and opened it for Dad to drive through. Once I closed the gate and got safely back in the car, we headed up a long, winding drive. A minute or so later, we stopped in front of a small but respectable house.

Screech.

Screech.

Screech.

The deafening insect chorus rang out even louder once the engine had been turned off.

"Is this really it?" asked Mum cautiously.

"Well," replied Dad, "there's only one way to find out."

He got out, stretched, and looked around. When no angry farmer or vicious dog appeared, he made his way up to the porch. At that point, I just couldn't stay put any longer.

"Get back in here at once," cried Mum as I jumped out of the car.

Too late. I ran off to join Dad at the front door.

Rat-a-tat-tat. No answer.

Rat-a-tat-tat. No answer.

"I hope this is the right address," sighed Mum under her breath. She had left the safety of the car to stand beside us, peering in through a window.

"Well," she said, "if this is Anne's place, she may have no idea that we're even here—I don't think she bothers to keep a calendar."

"I suppose that's true," replied Dad with a chuckle.

I suggested that we look for a key—there wasn't any point in knocking on the door of an empty house. After some hunting, Dad discovered one beneath a potted plant near the door. Luckily, it worked.

"So like her," said Mum dismissively. "We're supposed to guess where she leaves her keys."

The house definitely belonged to my aunt; a real mix of old and new furniture, grainy photographs, and wacky paintings filled it. On the kitchen table we found a note.

> *"Dear Leonard, Rachel, and my favorite young Luke,*
> *Make yourselves at home!*
> *In the fridge and freezer you'll find plenty of food, so please help yourselves. The tea is in the cupboard above the kettle, and there's a jar of ginger biscuits on the shelf next to the spice rack.*
> *I've had to attend to a neighbour who's got into a bit of trouble, but I shouldn't be away for more than a day. Please accept my sincerest apologies. (Life in these parts is a little unpredictable.)*
>
> *Lots of Love,*
> *Anne*
> *P.S. Gabriel, my farmhand, may be in tomorrow, so please don't be alarmed if you see a lovely old gentleman wandering about the property. If you have any questions, I'm sure he'd be more than willing to help."*

"Come on, Luke," said Dad with a wink, "I need a little help unpacking the car."

"Luke? Who's Luke?" I grumbled under my breath.

Mum decided that I wasn't allowed to go exploring until we

unpacked our clothes and ate dinner. Of course, it was dark by then—more like pitch-black—so I stood on the porch with Dad, gazing in awe at the stars. Millions of them filled the horizon from one end to the other. I'd never seen anything like it in my life.

"That," exclaimed Dad, "is precisely what the night sky should look like!"

And then, without hesitation, he launched into a lecture on finding North with the help of a few specific stars. I could never find those silly stars, which really frustrated him. The more I tried to listen, the sleepier I felt. Eventually, Mum came to my rescue.

"Leonard, shouldn't that boy be in bed by now? It's pretty late!"

And that was that. My day's journey ended on a strange pillow, in a strange house, beneath a beautiful but strange sky.

The following morning, once we'd cleaned up from breakfast—and after Mum had laid down her usual list of dos and don'ts—I finally managed to escape. It was time to explore the farm.

The front lawn wove past a rose garden and around some flowerbeds, before thinning out into a wood. I didn't see anything exciting, apart from a few overgrown areas where *who-knows-what* might lurk. Around the back, I stumbled upon a large, steel water tank resting on a rickety framework. A small dripping tap protruded from the side of the tank and, beneath that, a muddy puddle of water had collected. Fresh paw prints in the soil showed that some creature must have come for a drink the night before.

My mind raced. Could it have been a leopard, or maybe even a lion? I hadn't seen a dangerous creature in the wild before, but being out on an African farm must make it more likely. Still, I decided not to risk the woods on the first morning—it usually took a day or two before Mum relaxed enough to let me do my own thing.

The rest of the day passed by slowly. After lunch, Mum and Dad sat by the river on a small deck built in the shade of a willow tree. The riverbank looked interesting enough, so I set off to investigate a few rock pools. I waited, quiet and patient, until the shy inhabitants slowly emerged, one by one, from their hiding places. Large, lazy crabs came out to feed on algae along the waterline and, in the fine, glistening sand at the bottom, small catfish scavenged for food.

I tried, but I couldn't catch any of them. The crabs would jet into action as soon as my shadow fell across the water, disappearing with lightning speed into the crevices. The catfish also darted away, managing to stay hidden until I gave up the game. Eventually, I decided to explore elsewhere.

In the back garden, some way from the kitchen door, I came across a small dirt road—I was surprised that I hadn't seen it earlier in the morning. It came winding down from the hill, passed by the house, then went on towards the river and over an old stone bridge, before disappearing into a forest on the far side of the bank.

"Not always a wise decision to cross that bridge, my young friend!"

Surprised, I swung around to see who it was. An old man stood behind me wearing grubby blue overalls, a wide-rimmed hat, and earth-clogged boots. In his left hand he carried a spade, and his eyes had a certain sparkle about them.

"My name is Gabriel," he continued, "and you must be Luke."

"Cole, actually," I replied with mild frustration.

"Cole. Cole?" he repeated thoughtfully. "Anne never mentioned anyone by that name. Either way, you must be Leonard's son, right?"

"Yes," I replied, "Aunt Anne usually gets my name wrong."

"I see," he said with a knowing smile. "She's prone to mixing things up."

"What's wrong with crossing the bridge?" I asked.

But before Gabriel could answer, Dad called me in for supper.

"You'd better be going," suggested the old man. "It sounds like you're needed elsewhere."

"It was nice to meet you," I said as I made off, "and I hope we can talk another time."

On my way across the lawn, a faint meow drifted out from the bushes. I turned around to see a cat following me and couldn't resist stopping to say hello. The friendly animal came trotting up, wound itself around my legs, and purred loudly.

"Come on, Cole," called Dad, "let's not get distracted!"

"Shoo, shoo!" I exclaimed in vain. The cat followed me all the way to the kitchen door. What's more, it stayed outside the window while we ate dinner. I began to wonder if it belonged to Aunt Anne.

"That's highly unlikely," dismissed Mum. "If this is the cat's home, where are the food bowls?"

"True," agreed Dad, "and if we do let it in, we'll never be able to get rid of it. It's far better to leave the animal alone and hope it goes back to wherever it came from."

Later that evening, I lay in bed a little restless. What would I do for three whole weeks on an empty farm? Talk to Gabriel—if he was about? Take the cat on an adventure? Finally, when Mum and Dad had gone to sleep and the house was quiet, I decided to get out of bed.

Creak.

Clunk.

I opened the window and old rusted screen, letting in the sounds and smells of the cool night air. The moon hung full and motionless in the sky, flooding the garden in a silvery hue. From far beyond the house, perhaps in the woods, I heard the faint hooting of an owl. Just a few feet away, a small woodland mouse caught my attention as it scampered out from behind a large plant pot. With twitching whiskers, it paused briefly to sniff the air before scurrying away into the darkness. I loved the evening time; it felt so mysterious, transforming the sounds and shapes of the day into a whole new world. A quiver of excitement shot up my spine, and I felt an urge to climb out of the window. Hmm, what if Mum came in to check on me? I would never hear the end of it.

I climbed back into bed and drifted off to sleep.

Chapter Two

A Mysterious Invitation

═══○○○═══

Hmm, Hmm, Hmm
If I had one wish tonight,
I'd break these chains and take flight,
Then in this realm of pain and strife,
I'd free my soul and find new life.

But these chains aren't made of steel,
They're forged within, of pain unhealed.
Only a fool would not surrender,
For there, within, was once my splendor.

The eerie lyrics drifted in through the window, floated over the sheets, and tickled my ear. After some time, I pulled myself free from my dreams and realized that the song was real.

I felt a cool breeze wash over my cheek, then I remembered that I had left the window open. Quiet and still, I lay on my pillow, listening to the words as they trickled into the room. More than a song, the melody invited me, tugged me to discover where it came from. When it finally ended, I was torn between staying in bed, warm and safe, or following my curiosity.

Eventually I sat up and peered out into the night, looking for any sign of danger—an ominous shape or a subtle movement that spelled trouble. I saw nothing in the moonlight other than the silhouettes of a few garden shrubs. However, when I finally got out of bed and approached the window, my courage died. Perhaps sauntering off into the night was not the most responsible thing to do on an African farm.

Meow.

I was about to go back to sleep when the cat appeared, trotting out of the darkness.

"Oh dear, it's you again," I whispered with a smile.

Meow.

The inquisitive animal leapt up onto the window ledge, but, to my surprise, he didn't hang around for any attention. A second or two later, he jumped back into the garden and that's where he stayed, purring and meowing, inviting me to come outside.

In the end, I couldn't resist the temptation to join him, so I slipped out into the moonlight. At that moment, the song began again.

"That's coming from somewhere near the river," I said to myself.

Then I remembered the road that I'd discovered earlier in the day; it would be easy to follow it towards the edge of the farm. Sure, it wouldn't be wise to go all the way to the bridge, but at least I could get a little closer to the mysterious singer. Very carefully, I picked my way across the garden towards the road, pausing now and again to make sure that I didn't go too far from the house.

Crunch.

Crunch.

Crunch.

Each footstep on the gravel road echoed out through the still night air. I moved over onto the grass beside the road and kept going towards the river. Several yards later, I paused again.

"You're being stupid," said a little voice of caution in my head. "If Mum finds out, she'll probably ground you. Dad would be furious! You'd get a lecture on the importance of being *responsible*."

Despite these words, my curiosity rose up and tugged a little harder.

"You're nearly there!" it whispered. "Why turn back now?"

Taking a deep breath, I carried on.

I was right about the song coming from the direction of the river. In fact, the closer I got, the more it sounded like the singer was under the bridge. Something in the back of my memory stirred. Didn't Gabriel warn me about that bridge? And how would I find my way down the bank in the dark?

Lub-dub.

Lub-dub.

Lub-dub.

The power of the haunting melody grew stronger and stronger. Soon I found myself standing right at the edge of the river. I crouched down and peered at the hazy scene beneath the bridge. Beside a solid pillar, the figure of a young girl slowly came into focus. She looked about my age, or a little older. It wasn't easy to tell; I could only see a broken outline in the moonlight. But why would a girl be there, alone? Suddenly it dawned on me that she might not be alone at all.

I strained my eyes, searching for evidence of another person. Yes, there was something! Only a few feet away from her, I could see a large, motionless shape. Was it human? Or maybe a rock? My imagination ran wild; all sorts of peculiar monsters lurked in the shadows.

"Oh, stop it!" I whispered to myself. "Monsters don't exist!"

But the more I looked, the more certain I became that the shape was alive. Was that movement—maybe the gentle rise and fall of a breathing chest? And was that faint glint the reflection of an eye in the moonlight? Now and again, "it" even appeared to shuffle slightly. No, that wasn't a rock. Perhaps it was a large dog, maybe even a Great Dane?

Then I realized the cat had left my side. I panicked. The unpredictable little animal had kept me company, and his bright eyes and sensitive ears were good at picking up hidden dangers. I turned around slowly, scanning the road and garden. He was nowhere to be seen. Yet I stood there, stupidly peering beneath a bridge in the middle of the night, trying to see who or what was there. *Time to go home.*

I turned around and tiptoed away, following once again the verge of the road. When I was a fair distance from the bridge, I hopped onto the lawn and headed straight for my window.

Meow, came the soft plaintive cry of the cat.

"Some friend you are!" I whispered in reply. "Friendly enough to get me out of bed; not stupid enough to follow me all the way!"

Splat!

I sprawled face down on the ground. The cat had crossed my path, tripping me up. When I rolled over, the cheeky animal nudged me with his moist nose and scampered off. Picking myself up, I brushed off the grass, but the patches of dirt wouldn't budge.

"Great," I muttered under my breath. "How do I get these into the wash without Mum noticing?"

And where would I leave them to dry? Trying to hide them wouldn't work—Mum had an irritating habit of noticing these things. In the end, I decided to let tomorrow worry about itself. I climbed back in through the window and quietly crawled into bed. A little while later, before I fell asleep, the cat faithfully returned and sat purring on the window ledge.

I didn't sleep very well that night. A raging torrent of water threatened to wash me away, then a herd of bizarre creatures chased me into the kitchen. In one nasty dream after another, I had to remind myself that I was safe in my room. Not surprisingly, I got out of bed pretty late the next morning.

I knew exactly what I'd do that day. I threw on some clothes and snuck into the kitchen for a quick breakfast. After that, I slipped out of the house and made straight for the bridge.

In the light of day, I could see so much more than I had the night before. The riverbank formed a slight gorge as it descended towards the water's edge. It felt strange thinking that I had stood on that very spot a few hours earlier—things had appeared so much more mysterious in the quiet darkness.

Carefully, I picked my way down to the river, choosing a route that would be easy to follow when I returned that evening. My heart raced as I stepped into the cool, damp area beneath the bridge. A few feet from the water's edge, in a clearing in the sand, I found tracks. Someone had been there; I hadn't dreamt the whole thing up! And a little bit beyond that, I noticed a few more prints. Did the girl's dog leave those? If it was a dog.

I looked around, making a mental note of where the large rocks and holes were. The more quietly I arrived that night, the better. There could be no dithering, slipping, or muddied clothes the second time around.

For the rest of the day, the promise of adventure that night totally consumed me. Maybe I was foolish to hope to see the girl in the same place again, but I made my plans anyway. I would need a warm sweater, old running shoes, jeans, and a good flashlight. I could collect all that easily enough. Dad had given me a flashlight as a gift—I had used it when we unpacked the car on our first night.

And, since Mum didn't suspect anything yet, I just had to hide my muddy pajamas until the following day.

That night, after helping to clear the table and clean up the kitchen, I went to bed early. Mum knocked on the door and came quietly into the room.

"How are things going, Cole? Are you enjoying yourself?"

"Yes, thanks," I replied.

"You're off to bed pretty early tonight."

"I'm a little tired. It's been a long day."

"OK, but you will let us know if you get bored or lonely?"

"Yes, Mum. Good night."

"Good night, Cole."

A little while later, when all was quiet, I jumped out of bed and opened the window. When would I hear the mysterious melody?

"She probably won't be there tonight," I mumbled. "I'm sitting here for nothing."

Before I could finish the thought, however, the eerie song made its way into my room once again—gentle, and so inviting.

I looked at my watch and decided to wait a little longer; I had to make sure that Mum and Dad were asleep. After a while, I changed into my clothes, slipped out of the window, and made my way to the river's edge. Now and again, I paused to listen. The melody seemed to be coming from the same direction as it had last night. About halfway down the road, the cat bounded out of the darkness and joined the investigation, arriving with eyes and ears on full alert.

"You need a name, my clever friend," I whispered quietly. "I think I'll call you Pebbles from now on, if that's OK with you?"

And Pebbles did appear to be clever; he knew exactly where I was going. As we approached the river, I slowed my pace to a cautious tiptoe, and he crouched right down, as if stalking a bird. We came to a dead stop at the riverbank.

Full of anticipation, I squatted down to look under the bridge. At first I considered using my flashlight, until I realized that shining a light would draw attention. No, I'd keep the flashlight for emergencies only. I focused my eyes as hard as I could until I recognized the hazy outline of the girl with the same large form beside her. It shuffled slightly and twitched from time to time. What on earth was it?

A load of fears wormed their way into my imagination. My mission felt far too reckless, even dangerous. Pebbles remained crouching in the grass a few paces to the right. Did he know something that I didn't? Was I about to be eaten by a weird beast? My courage dwindled; I stood up slowly and turned around to walk back home.

"Are you going to leave without saying hello?"

I froze on the spot. Had the girl spoken? Was I dreaming?

"Uh…" was all I could manage.

Pebbles sat up, staring at the riverbed with fixed curiosity.

"You don't have to be afraid," the girl assured me. "My name is Riola."

"My…my name is Cole," I spluttered with some effort.

"Hello, Cole!"

"H-hello, your song was very…beautiful. I came down to see who—"

"Actually," she interrupted, "you came last night, too, but you didn't have the courage to say hello."

"Oh, ah…I mean…yes, I did come last night." She'd caught me off guard.

"Well, are you going to come and say hello this time?"

"Err, of course," I answered nervously, "or…you could always come up here?"

"If you'd prefer that. Are you frightened of the river?"

"Uh, no, there's just a little more light up here."

Before I could say another word, Riola scrambled up the bank and stood before me. Thin and unkempt, she wore tattered clothes and a heartwarming smile. And yes, she was probably a little older than me, which I'd guessed when I saw her the night before. Although she was friendly enough, she glanced about nervously, almost as if she expected someone to be following her. That made me anxious.

"Don't worry," she said, "he won't hurt you."

"Uh, who won't hurt me?"

"Humphrey," she replied.

"Humphrey?" I repeated with slight trepidation.

"Yes, my friend Humphrey. You must have seen him last night; he was sitting right beside me."

"Um, and Humphrey is a…?"

"A troll," she answered, completing my sentence for me.

My eyes widened and my mouth nearly dropped open.

"Yes. Right. Humphrey, your…your troll."

Could I have slipped into a dream? I looked back towards the house. It was still there. Yes, this was reality, strange as it might be. Pebbles, completely unbothered, rose to his feet and stood looking up at Riola.

"Hello, kitty!" she said, leaning down to give him some attention. Pebbles collapsed into her hand, in his element. Purring loudly, he rolled onto his back, exposing his soft underbelly.

"What a lovely cat you have!" she said with delight.

"Um…I'm not sure he is my cat," I replied. "I think he may belong to Aunt Anne."

"The owner of the farm?" she inquired.

"That's right. Have you seen her before?"

"From time to time. The cat is gorgeous either way, and so trusting!"

"Yes, he is very trusting. I've named him Pebbles."

"That suits him perfectly!" she exclaimed, smothering the little animal with affection.

At that point, I suddenly realized that I'd lost track of the time. Had I been away for an hour? Two? Could it have been more?

"Riola, I think I'd better be going back home."

"So soon?"

"Afraid so, I've been out here for a while now and, well, I don't want my parents to be worried."

"OK," she sighed. "Will you visit us tomorrow?"

"Us? You mean, you and the troll."

"Yes, Humphrey and I," she answered. "He's no harm at all. I think you'll find that he's really quite shy."

"Yes, of course," I said, trying to be brave. "I'd love to meet Humphrey."

"Thank you!" she exclaimed.

Riola climbed back down the bank and disappeared into the darkness.

For a few moments I stood exactly where I was; I couldn't quite believe that I had met the mysterious girl. And what about the troll? I would definitely have to keep that to myself. The hooting of a nearby owl reminded me once again of the time, and I quickly made my way up the road and across the lawn. As I climbed back into my room, I spotted Pebbles trailing up the path. That night, I let him sleep at the foot of my bed.

The following morning, I woke up late and full of hay fever. Before my sneezing attracted Mum's attention, I let the cat out of the window. More than happy to jump into the day with his usual gusto, he leapt away as Mum knocked on the door and came into my room.

"Wow, Cole, you're congested today, aren't you? Perhaps there's too much pollen in the air for your sinuses?"

"Perhaps," I replied cautiously.

"Did you remember your medicine?"

"Yes, Mum, I remembered my medicine."

I did have slightly irritable sinuses, as well as a tight chest from time to time. It was nothing serious, but Mum insisted that I take my medication everywhere I went—very annoying!

I spent the rest of the day with Dad and the gentle Gabriel, working on various chores around the farm. Dad was thrilled to find a broken-down vintage truck in the garage. He loved old cars even more than he loved the stars, and could tinker away for hours. As for me, whenever we stopped to take a break, my mind drifted back to the river's edge.

That afternoon, Gabriel announced that he was leaving for his annual holiday. Before he walked down the drive, I sidled up to him, hoping to carry on our conversation from the night before.

"What's with the stone bridge?" I asked.

"Well," smiled the old man, "some say that, from time to time, those who cross it enter a foreign land."

"What!" I gasped. "Is it true?"

"Your Aunt Anne is convinced," he replied, "and I have reason to believe that she may be right. It could be the bridge, or even the river—either way, there's something different about those banks. If I were you, I'd be very cautious about visiting them."

He said good-bye and went on his way.

I hadn't told him about Riola, or her troll, and it occurred to me that, if his story were true, then perhaps she had come from an unknown land. My mind whirred with possibilities.

"Cole," yelled Dad from the garage, "where are you?"

The sound of my name pulled me back into reality, and I ran off to help with the old truck.

Towards the late afternoon, we had an early dinner together on the deck beside the river. Considering Gabriel's words of caution, I wondered if we should eat in the kitchen, but Mum had already laid out the cold meats, salads, and breads. It soon became obvious that we weren't used to the territory. Legions of mosquitoes rose up from the cooling rock pools and bombarded our ankles and necks. Eventually, Mum, certain she'd seen a bottle of insect repellent earlier in the day, went into the house to get it. It worked and, with the mosquitoes gone, we sat down to enjoy our food.

Somewhere in the conversation, Dad mentioned that if Aunt Anne didn't turn up by the following morning, then we should probably try and find out what had become of her.

"Darn," I grumbled under my breath, "that'll stop me from seeing Riola again."

When we had finished eating, my curiosity led me down the river for one last exploration before sundown. If there really was something about that bridge, then who knew what I might discover?

Chapter Three

The Disappearance

=○○○=

As I got closer to the bridge, the familiar sound of Riola's song caught me by surprise—I hadn't expected her to be out before dark.

When I reached the bank, I leaned over the edge to call her. As I opened my mouth, I heard her voice.

"Good evening, Cole!"

How did she do that? Once again she was a step ahead.

"Hello, Riola. You're out early."

"Sometimes early, sometimes late, sometimes not at all," she answered. "Would you like to come down and say hello to Humphrey?"

"Uh…yes…of course I would," I replied cautiously.

I had no way out. Then I noticed Pebbles on the other side of the river, sleeping on the top of a boulder well away from the water. Stretched out in complete surrender, he caught the last of the day's sunlight. Surely, if Pebbles felt safe near the troll, then the troll had already eaten. Nevertheless, I was still petrified—but I didn't want Riola to know that. Then I remembered Mum and Dad; if anything did go wrong, they weren't far away. Feeling a little more at ease, I climbed down the bank and into the gorge beneath the bridge.

Riola sat next to Humphrey on a large patch of sand a couple of feet from the water's edge, the same place they had been the night before. Humphrey seemed to be fast asleep.

"Is he resting?" I asked.

"Yes," she replied, "trolls prefer to sleep during the day. He'll wake up when the sun's gone down and the moon's out."

That was a relief; I guessed that I would be safe for at least another hour.

I leaned over to take a closer look at the troll. Humphrey was definitely large, perhaps the size of a fully grown male pig. He lay grunting quietly, with his legs twitching every so often. I tried to get a glimpse of his face, but he had tucked it under a paw—or was that a trotter? I could only see an enormous ear protruding into the air.

"I bet he could hear someone from a mile off," I said in awe.

"Haven't you ever seen a troll?" asked Riola.

"Nope, never. I didn't think they were real."

"Didn't think they were real? Are you being serious?"

"Afraid so; I thought they belonged in fables."

"Well, if you're going to hang around this time, you may as well sit down and get to know us."

I made my way to a flat rock and got comfortable. As I did, Riola's expression glazed over, and the conversation came to an abrupt halt. She gazed out into the sky, watching a small flock of birds dart here and there. It felt rather awkward. As the silence continued, I became aware of a dark mass of shapes behind Humphrey.

"Ah, Riola…is Humphrey your only troll?"

"No," she replied, "I have three in all, but don't let that bother you."

She stared out into the sky again, but her frank, casual reply made my worries fade away. Besides, I wasn't going to ask if I could have a closer look at the others; being introduced to one troll a day was more than enough for a beginner.

"I've been thinking about something," I said later.

"Mm-hmm," she mumbled.

"How did you come to be here?"

"You mean," she answered, "where are my parents?"

"Well…yes," I replied quietly.

It certainly wasn't the best way to start a conversation—I probably should've picked another topic. Anyway, I'd asked the question now. Riola sat up and looked at me with her distant, unsettled eyes.

"I come from somewhere quite far away," she began, her eyes a little moist. "Mama, Papa, and I lived in a small village on the side of a hill by the sea. Papa was a fisherman, he was gone for most of the day, and Mama used to run a little shop. In the afternoon, after school, I'd go exploring with my friends through the alleyways of our village and all along the hilly coastline. We found wildflowers when the spring and summer rains came, and watched flocks of bright little birds chatter in the bushes. In autumn and winter, the sky would be bright blue and clear. I miss those walks, and I miss the times when Mama would come with us, and we'd talk for hours."

Riola's story intrigued me, but before I could ask any questions, she changed the subject.

"Cole," she whispered, "have you ever crossed this bridge? Have you ever walked into the forest on the other side?"

"Well, I thought about it, but someone told me it's not a wise thing to do."

"I suppose you're right. You could end up in another world—perhaps even the world I come from. It's not always that way; most of the time you'd probably find yourself on the other side of the river."

"Yep, that's pretty much what Aunt Anne's farmhand told me. So, what's the name of the land where you come from?"

"Geltonia," she replied, "and that isn't the only place near your world. There are other lands too, like Morodia or even Khülm."

"Really! What about the trolls? Do they come from Geltonia, or somewhere else?"

"They come from Khülm, and strange beasts are merely the beginning of it for anyone who ends up there. Khülm is a completely different world."

Now, if it weren't for Humphrey, Riola would have come across as little more than a good storyteller. Yet, deep inside, I felt more and more sure that there was something very different about this girl. It was obvious really. Who would spend their time singing beneath a bridge in the dead of night, enjoying the company of three trolls?

"Mama became very ill," she said, returning to her story. "The illness wouldn't go away, and after eight months she…she died."

Riola hung her head, trying to fight back a stream of tears.

"At first, Dad was really angry, and I was scared to be with him, but then a deep sadness overcame him. Early one morning, about two months after Mama died, he got into his boat and rowed out to sea. I never…I never saw him again. I was terrified…so terrified. Thankfully, a kind neighbor took me in and looked after me. A little while later, Aunt Urella arrived. She said I was to go and live with her high up in the mountains. I hadn't met Aunt Urella before, and I don't really think that she wanted to look after me. My friends said that the mountain people were different from us, and they were right. The place where she lived was nothing like what I was used to."

Riola turned her head to the sky and paused. Once she had gathered her courage, she carried on.

"Aunt Urella had two sons, Urmill and Verdon—they were really nasty. My uncle, Aunt Urella's husband, hardly ever came home. The neighbors used to say that he had a wandering spirit. One morning, Aunt Urella took me to a market in another town. Urmill and Verdon came along, too."

For just a moment, Riola's eyes lit up.

"It was great—a huge, colorful place, throbbing with all sorts of people. I had seen nothing like it in all my life. People bustled about yelling and bartering, selling fish, meat, clothes, jewelry, and more things than I could count."

She told the story of her life, sometimes staring out into the sky and sometimes gazing across the river, but never making eye contact. I sat in complete silence and learned a lot about my new friend.

That day, she had wandered off into the market with Urmill and Verdon and, being the type of boys they were, they played a silly game and hid from her. Riola panicked and ran around trying to find them, but she failed and got terribly lost. By evening time she still hadn't found anyone she knew, so a family took her in and promised to look after her for the night. She didn't know that they were a family of thieves.

Lost in a foreign place, without money and without parents, it's easy to trust someone who offers to help you—even when you know you probably shouldn't. Cunning as they were, the family sold Riola to slave traders, and the slave traders took her far away to a land called Gorr. They sold her off again, this time to a mine. Deep down underground, where no one cared about a soul, she was forced to work long, grueling hours.

I wanted to know many more details about her story, but she couldn't tell me everything that day. And, as time marched on, I recognized the twittering of the night birds. The sun had almost set.

"Oh darn!" I exclaimed, jumping to my feet. "How late is it?"

Riola stopped mid-sentence. "I'm not too sure, Cole. Do you have to leave now?"

"Yes, I do!" I replied in panic. "I should get back and let Mum and Dad know that I'm alright. I hope they haven't been looking for me."

"Goodbye, Cole," said Riola. "I hope to see you soon."

"Sure. You will," I replied, scrambling up the riverbank.

When I climbed the stairs to the deck, I didn't see my parents anywhere. I figured that they had gone back into the house. Then I saw it.

The folding chairs had been knocked over and lay scattered on their sides.

"That's not like Dad," I said to myself, worried. "He wouldn't have left those outside."

I leaned over the rail, scanning the riverbank, then spotted the picnic basket bobbing up and down in the water a few feet from the shore. An evening bird fluttered down and landed on it for a few seconds, twittered with curiosity, and then flew off.

Something odd must have happened.

I ran up to the house and burst through the kitchen door, calling, "Mum? Dad?"

There was no reply. The house was cool, dark, and quiet.

Did something happen with the river? Did Aunt Anne come back?

I turned on the lights and searched everywhere, running from room to room in growing desperation. I found no clues, not even a note left by the phone. I grabbed my flashlight and hastily searched the garden, starting in the front near the driveway. Our hired car remained where it always had been; it hadn't moved.

As quickly as I could, I worked my way around to the back where the water tank stood. *Drip, drip, drip.* I heard nothing but the tap as I stopped to catch my breath. The smell of fresh mint rose up from the herb patch that grew around the permanent puddle. I still saw no sign of any activity.

My thoughts raced at ninety miles an hour. Had Aunt Anne dragged my parents off on some wild goose chase without giving them time to collect me? That couldn't be; surely Mum would've protested. And besides, Dad was far too levelheaded to go off into the night with his eccentric sister. Perhaps a neighbor, or even the police, had hauled them off to help rescue her. They might not have had the time to leave a note, and that would explain the overturned chairs.

There must have been a panic; I could almost visualize the scene. *A police car arrives with a screech; an officer jumps out and yells something. Mum and Dad look shocked. They stand up and tear across the lawn, hop into the vehicle and are driven off.*

Yes, something way out of the ordinary had happened. It could've been Aunt Anne or the river, but, either way, there was no time to dither. I needed help. There wasn't a phonebook anywhere, only a small piece of paper on the fridge with a few contacts scribbled on it. Aunt Anne's writing was almost impossible to read. I could only decipher two numbers: one for the local police, and the other for a friend, Camilla. *Try the friend first,* I thought. I lifted the receiver and dialed. It rang, and rang, and rang.

Great, they're out. I'll try the police.

I had no idea what I was going to say, but I lifted the receiver again and dialed. It rang a few times, made a clicking sound, and then a recorded message played. The line was very feint—I couldn't make out what was being said. I hung up and tried again, but it was no better.

Pointless. This would happen to me. There's only one thing left to do.

I charged into my room, grabbed a sweater and set off into the night. Before I left, I decided to leave the porch and kitchen lights on—in case Mum and Dad did come home later. Then I tore off into the back garden, slamming the door closed as I left. I had decided to brave the night with Riola. I wanted company so badly that I was even prepared to face her trolls.

As I scrambled across the lawn, I heard a familiar meow from Pebbles, who pounced out of the darkness.

"Not now," I spluttered as the excited cat leapt across my path. I needed to make it back down to the bridge before Riola moved off for the night. She had been there earlier than usual that day, and I worried that she might have already left.

When I arrived at the bridge, I peered over the edge of the bank and aimed my light into the shallow gorge beneath. Nothing. The light fell on the empty stone where I'd been sitting an hour or so earlier.

"Silly, silly me," I muttered with frustration. "I sat there too long. Now look what's happened."

Pebbles nudged me, full of curiosity and completely unaware of my panic. Then it dawned on me. Riola probably made her way across the bridge and into the forest. For some reason, I knew that she wouldn't have travelled into the farmlands on our side of the river. No, she would head for secret places where she could hide with her trolls. The choice seemed impossible: cross the bridge into the dark woods in search of her or stay alone on an isolated farm in the African wilderness.

CHAPTER FOUR:

The Heavy, Silent Darkness

═○○○═

I clearly remembered Gabriel's caution concerning the bridge: *Some say that, from time to time, those who cross it enter a foreign land.*

"If worst comes to worst," I asked myself, "could it really be so bad on the other side?"

Riola came from another land, and she seemed pretty normal. Then again, if I dared to cross, would I be able to return? Wouldn't it be safer to stay on the farm? One night alone wouldn't be that bad, surely?

But what if Mum and Dad didn't return the following day? What if they didn't return at all?

Finally, the terrifying thought of being left alone got the better of me. I literally charged across the bridge. On the other side, I stopped dead still. The air was eerily quiet. A cool breeze blew around my feet and trailed off down the river. In the branches of the trees, somewhere high above, a large bird let out a cry and flew away into the night. From the opposite bank of the river, Pebbles peered at me, meowed, and then bounded off into the garden.

I looked around and saw the road ahead with the shadowy forest to my left and right. Was some dark creature watching me? Would a troll hunt me down?

"Get a grip!" I exclaimed under my breath. "It's just a normal forest."

The dirt road I stood on seemed pretty normal, too, and it appeared to be well used. There wasn't anything unusual or wild about the trees, either. Yes, the air felt strangely quiet, but it was a forest after all. And, even in the night, the full moon provided enough light to see obvious shapes. All in all, it felt like any other evening. Perhaps Gabriel had exaggerated. Feeling a little less anxious, I shone my light up the road and set off to find Riola.

After a few minutes of running, I stopped to get my bearings. The bridge lay far behind; I had entered the deep heart of the forest, and the surrounding trees seemed enormous. Layer upon layer of branches reached up through dizzy heights into the night sky. Dense darkness shrouded the chilly air—even the silvery moonlight could barely penetrate the trees now. I could only hear the steady sound of my own breathing, and the quick pulsations of my heart. I glanced about nervously, trying to work out how far I should go. What if I didn't find Riola after all?

Beaming my light around, I carefully scanned the road ahead. It climbed upwards for a short distance, then disappeared around a sharp bend. I decided that I would run until I could see around the bend. If I heard or saw anything that could be Riola, I would keep going. But if nothing was there, I would go back to the farm.

I jogged up the hill at a fair pace. At the bend, I decided to lower my light and keep the beam only a few feet ahead. If anything ominous was lurking about, I certainly didn't want to catch its attention.

Swoosh!

Whirl.

Cree-eack…

Whirl.

Swoosh!

A strong wind gusted, swirling its way through the trees. The eerie sound of whistling air and groaning branches broke my nerve. I swung around to head for home as fast as I could go. At that exact moment, I heard a distinct *clink*.

A gentle but definite clinking sound drifted out from somewhere ahead. I paused midflight and held my breath, listening carefully. Yes, there it was again! Perhaps it was a gate knocking back and forth in the wind? The sound grew quieter. Was it moving away? I trotted up the road a little further, and the clinking grew louder. It was moving—were Riola and her trolls just ahead of me? Filled with curiosity and hope, I regained my courage and set off in pursuit. The sound grew more and more audible with every step that I took. "This meeting could be interesting," I said to myself. "If it *is* her, I'll probably give her the fright of her life."

"Hello, Cole!"

I nearly jumped out of my skin. However, before the impulse to flee kicked in, I realized that it was Riola.

How does she do that? I wondered. *She's always one step ahead.*

"Hello, Riola," I said, trying to catch my breath.

"You're a long way from home!" she exclaimed. "What are you doing out here?"

"Well, I was hoping to find you," I replied. "I think something strange has happened to my parents. They're…missing."

"Yes, I know; they've gone missing, all right."

"Huh? What do you mean by that?"

"They were swallowed," she answered coolly.

"Swallowed! Swallowed by what?"

"Shyla," she replied, without offering any further details.

"What? Who—what is Shyla?"

"Shyla is a large creature that lives in the river. You'd call her a python, but she's no snake, she's a water serpent."

Riola, who had seemed feisty earlier, but by no means uncaring, now sounded completely blasé about the situation. I was utterly bewildered.

"Don't worry," she went on, "Shyla will spit your parents out soon enough. A bit of a strange creature, that one; she often eats people and then coughs them up a week or so later. I think humans disagree with her stomach."

"And if she does spit them out, will my mum and dad still be alive?"

"More than likely. People don't seem to die inside her. How that works is beyond me, so don't ask. At worst, they'll be a little disheveled and confused. That's about it."

From trolls to man-eating serpents—I struggled to work out whether or not I was dreaming.

"And you know for sure that Mum and Dad were eaten by her?"

"Yep, afraid so," answered Riola. "She's been around the shores of that farmhouse for a while now. If you had spent any time near the riverbank, she would've been there, attracted by your movement. In fact, while we were talking under the bridge, she glided past—I don't think you saw the flicker in the water. She's usually lazy, but with food on her mind, she moves like lightening."

"You were lucky to have been chatting with me," she continued. "If you had stayed with your parents, you could've ended up in her belly, too!"

It was all too much; I was tired, hungry, and overwhelmed. The world went blank.

A little while later, I awoke to a gentle rocking motion. When I opened my eyes, a myriad of twinkling stars, all scattered across the heavens, came into focus. I was flat on my back, lying on something that moved at a steady, rhythmic pace. Feeling the first hint of panic, I tried to get up, but couldn't. I'd been tied down with a rope. People say to keep calm when a crisis hits, so I tried to lie quietly and listen for any clues that would tell me where I was. Sure enough, I heard a clinking sound and muffled footsteps.

Are those Riola's footsteps? And there's that metallic knocking sound again. Yes, it's either Riola, or I've been caught by thieves.

Panic swirled through my body. What had I got myself into?

"Riola?" I eventually called out in desperation.

"Not so loud!" came the abrupt reply. I recognized Riola's voice and sighed with relief.

"Steady now, Humphrey," she said quietly, "I'd better untie him."

Humphrey? Did I hear that right? Had I been tied to the back of a troll?

The rocking motion stopped, and I felt myself being lowered. There was a loud huff, a grunt, and then a shuffling sound as Riola undid the ropes that bound me. With my body freed from the troll's back, I leapt to the ground and looked about.

"Where are we? Is this still the same road?"

"Yes, it's the same road, but don't talk so loudly!" scolded Riola a second time. "You're going to have to learn to lower your voice; we don't want to attract any attention."

"Sorry, I'll try to be quieter. Tell me, what exactly are you afraid of? Do you get thugs around here?"

"Yes, and slave traders, too," she snapped. "Plenty of them are out at night—their kind don't work during the day. Besides that, there's a whole host of creatures on the prowl for an easy meal."

"So…ah…we're in a different land?"

"You're in Khülm," she answered with a frown.

"Huh? Khülm? Are you being serious?"

"Yes, I'm afraid so," she replied. "Remember, even you knew that the bridge might take you to another land. Well, it has, and you're lucky to have arrived in the one I'm in. Come now, we need to get going."

"But where exactly is Khülm? How safe is it?"

"You're here now, Cole. There's no point in worrying about the details of where Khülm is or how safe you are."

"What? Are you mad? I'm not going a step further. I don't have to be here. I have a home, and I can go back to it if I want."

"Keep your voice down!" whispered Riola. "Khülm lies next to Geltonia, but it's not safe. It's not safe at all. Didn't I just say that there are slave traders about? Does that sound safe to you? And no, Cole, you can't just go home. Even if you did find that bridge again, there's no saying where it would take you."

A cold chill went down my spine. My tongue went dry, and my legs felt weak.

"I have to…I have to…find home," I stammered. "There's no way I can stay here."

"Well, there's no way I'm staying here either," said Riola. "I may be able to get you back to your aunt's house, but it will take some time. Right now, we need to keep quiet and get moving. We're not safe on this road."

"So, I can get home, right?"

"Perhaps, but like I said, it won't happen quickly. You're going to have to get used to Khülm for a while."

"Ah…how long is a while?"

There was no answer. Riola was clearly irritable, so I decided to keep the questions for later and stay close by her side. Things had gone from bad to worse, and I wasn't going anywhere on my own.

"Did I faint earlier on?" I asked a little later. "How on earth did I end up on Humphrey's back?"

"Well, I'm not sure if you fainted," she replied. "You certainly collapsed, and then fell straight into a deep sleep. You were out for about an hour. I'm sorry for tying you to Humphrey, but I didn't think it would be right to leave you in the road."

"Thank you." I smiled nervously. Inside, I wondered if I should have gone looking for Riola after all.

My eyes struggled to adjust to the heavy darkness—waking up in the belly of a whale probably wouldn't have been much different. Without thinking, I looked for my flashlight. Sure enough, I found it in one of my pockets—Riola must have put it there before binding me onto Humphrey's back. I pulled it out and briefly shone it around to see if anything lurked nearby.

"Put that darn thing away!" she whispered irritably.

Suddenly aware of my stupidity, I switched it off and shoved it back in my pocket.

"Look, Cole," she said firmly, "if you carry on like this, I'm going to ask you to leave us alone. You could bring some serious harm our way. No lights, no loud talking. Got it?"

"I'm sorry…I wasn't thinking…"

"And the trolls are very sensitive to light," she continued, almost ignoring my apology, "so don't ever shine that thing at them either. Give it a little time and your eyes will adapt to the darkness."

"What's that clinking noise?" I asked, trying to change the topic. "I'm sure that's the sound I followed when I caught up with you earlier."

"It's the trolls," she replied. "A long chain keeps them together; you can hear the links scraping along the ground. Don't let it worry you; that type of noise will scare off the lone brigands and smaller wild animals. They'll think we're hunters or soldiers. And anyway, if they did get too close, Humphrey would have them running. It's the organized slave traders that we really have to watch out for. If any of them are nearby and they overhear us talking, they'll know we're kids. We'd fetch a good price on the market, and the trolls wouldn't be able to defend us—they'd probably be caught and sold too."

"Oh wow, that sounds awful. I'll be sure to whisper from now on. Tell me, why do you keep the trolls in chains? Isn't that a bit cruel?"

Without any reply, she turned and walked off slowly up the road—clearly, my question had offended her. I lost no time in following. The possibility of being left alone was too petrifying.

Into the night we continued, climbing higher and higher with each step. My eyes eventually adjusted to the lack of light, and I could see more and more detail in the branches of the trees. All that time, Riola did not say a word, making the silence of the forest seem even worse. I could only hear the creaking of the trees, the shuffling of feet, and the clinking of the trolls' chain. At one point, she passed me a small blanket, which I wrapped around my shoulders. The air had gone from chilly to very cold, and I was grateful for the extra warmth.

The further we walked, the more questions plagued me.

Is it foolish to trust her?

Where are we headed?

Will I ever see my parents again?

Then, unexpectedly, something distracted me from my fears. In the branches high above, I heard a quiet fluttering. The sound didn't really bother me, but the strange feeling that it had been there for quite some time did. Were we being followed? I turned around and let the others go slightly ahead. Then, without Riola noticing, I briefly flashed my light into the trees. The beam landed on an enormous black bird, which swooped off the moment it had been exposed. I didn't have the courage to tell Riola about it—confessing that I had used my light again would only have made her bad mood worse.

"I'm bushed," I said a little while later. "Are we ever going to get some sleep?"

"Yes, I suppose so," she mumbled. "It must be way past *your* bedtime."

"It is. Would you mind telling me where we're going?"

"I will tell you," she answered, "but first, let's find somewhere to rest for the night. Scouting out the right place can be tricky. We can't camp on the side of the road. Too many thieves and smugglers use this route. We'd be sitting ducks."

She walked up to Humphrey and whispered something into his ear. Humphrey grunted. All three trolls stopped in their tracks. With his moist, twitching nose lifted high into the air, he swayed gently from side to side, scanning the night breeze for a scent. Very soon he detected something and went blundering off through the trees. The other two trolls quickly followed; a mass of lumbering shapes and a long, heavy chain plowing through the foliage. Riola and I stayed close behind. Neither of us wanted to get lost in the darkness.

Crackle.

Scrape.

Snap.

Scratch!

We plowed deeper and deeper into the forest. Soon we'd left the road at least a quarter of a mile behind us. Thorns pulled at my shirt, small twigs got caught in my socks, and piles of mush and rotten leaves climbed up past my ankles.

"Oh darn!" I grumbled to myself. "Why didn't I bring a change of clothes?"

"Stop!" came the abrupt sound of Riola's voice. We had stumbled into a clearing. The large, open space was, except for a layer of soft, wet grass, free from all growth. Here, the oppressive darkness of the forest gave way to the gentle light of the moon. On the far side, the upper ridge of a rocky cliff rose sharply into the air.

It would be risky to cross the open space without the protection of the trees or the cover of darkness. Riola and I remained on the edge of the clearing. The trolls came to a dead stop, their ears and noses alert and twitching. Humphrey ventured out first, the chain pulling the other two trolls behind him. When nothing reacted to the trolls, we caught up with them. The trolls made a beeline for the foot of the cliff, where I saw Humphrey's silhouette shuffle a little to the right and then disappear.

"He's found it!" whispered Riola.

"Found what?" I asked.

"A cave!" she replied. "I send Humphrey off to find caves— there're more than a few in these parts. Some are *fairly* safe to sleep in. If you're lucky enough to find the right one, there might be a load of tasty mushrooms, too. Hopefully, it'll also be deep and dark, so we can rest there until late tomorrow afternoon. Travelling in the midday sun damages a troll's eyes."

"OK Riola, I get the part about too much light being bad for your pets, but why are the caves 'fairly safe' to sleep in?"

"Oh…don't worry about that, Cole. Let's catch up with Humphrey, or we'll be left in the cold."

She ran after the trolls, and I followed, desperate to keep up.

The mouth of the cave, a jagged, vertical crack in the rock face, lay slightly to the right of a grove of trees. Once inside, Riola rummaged about in a bag tied to one of the trolls. It was pitch black, and despite having nimble hands, she struggled to find her tinderbox. After that, trying to coax a flame into life was almost impossible.

"What about using my flashlight?" I asked. "It won't last forever, but it'll make things easier while you try get a flame going."

"OK, fine," she answered. "But shine it over my hands only, because…"

"Yes, I know, it's bright and it'll shock the trolls."

Eventually, with a lot of hard work, her lantern glowed warmly and my flashlight, with its cheap batteries, faded away. In the flickering light, we could see a sprawling network of tunnels. Each led off from the main cavern, twisted through a few turns, and then disappeared into the heart of the mountain. The air was stagnant, damp, and cold. Flowing lines and deep contours swirled across every surface, as if once, far back in time, water had surged through the cave before pouring out into the forest. A rich deposit of fine sand covered the floor. I bent down and trailed my fingers through it. Yes, it was a comfy place to settle down, nice and soft, but were we really going to spend the night in an eerie cave?

"Riola, how safe is it in here? And be honest."

"The trolls will pick up on anything threatening," she replied. "As long as they seem peaceful, we'll be OK."

For the first time since our journey began, I got a real glimpse of the trolls. The three of them peered at me briefly before shuffling off to find mushrooms. They did walk upright, but their hunched posture looked uncomfortable. Riola told me that they could move with speed if they needed to. Their front paws were small and nimble, similar to the hands of a monkey. Their eyes, little more than black beads, couldn't have been good for much, despite their sensitivity to light. Their ears, on the other hand, were enormous, and their noses were long, supple, and forever twitching. I couldn't help glancing at the huge tusks on either side of their mouths; Humphrey's were by far the largest.

I stayed where I was, watching them snort and forage about the cave. Riola came and joined me.

"Funny," I said quietly, "they look like they could be dangerous, but here they are, calmly eating plants."

"Some species are very dangerous," she cautioned. "Never take a troll for granted. Few are tame like mine."

"Oh. Right. Thanks for the warning. Tell me, what have you named them? I know Humphrey, but what about the other two?"

"They're Bella and Mrs. P. Bella's the overweight one, and definitely the most sluggish—she loves her food far too much! Mrs. P is the moody one of the bunch. She's small, quiet, and melancholy, but very faithful."

"They're so awkward—almost comical," I said with a smile.

"I know," replied Riola. "They're easily misunderstood. It's their quirky features, I suppose. Just don't make the mistake of thinking that they're stupid."

"No, I never meant that. Where did you meet them?"

"In the mines; it's a long story, best kept for another time."

She blew a deep, long whistle. The trolls stopped their foraging and lumbered their way back to us, sniffing, snorting, and tasting the air as they went.

"This is where we'll sleep tonight," she announced. "Not too far within the chambers, but not in the open, either. The mouth of the cave is perfect. That leaves us room to sneak deeper if needed, or to flee into the forest. The aim is to avoid getting cornered; you can never be too sure which direction a threat may come from."

The trolls sniffed the ground intently as they searched for a place to settle, turning repeatedly in tight circles, and padding the ground with their feet.

"Mum had a dog that used to do that," I said, feeling a little homesick.

"They're being picky," replied Riola. "It's a new place every night, which isn't the best for them."

Reaching into a bag, she pulled out two oblong shapes.

"What are those?" I asked.

"Nasty dried roots," she answered with a smile. "The trick is to try and ignore the taste. Believe it or not, they're good for you."

Cautiously, I bit into one of them. She hadn't been joking about the sour taste, but I felt too hungry to complain. After our simple meal, we drank from a water bottle and then settled down on the soft, sandy cave floor. Riola offered me a large, thick, grubby blanket, good for keeping out the chilly air.

I was scared that night. After all, this was my first outdoor experience in a true wilderness. What's more, I was in a wilderness in Khülm, a completely foreign land notorious for its many dangers. I tried my best to get comfortable and clung to the hope of finding Mum and Dad. *I will make my way back*, I thought to myself. *It's not impossible. I will get home.*

In the end, fear loosened its hold on me and exhaustion took over. I drifted off to sleep.

Chapter Five:

A Creature from the Deep
=○◯○=

Hisss.

At first, I thought the peculiar sound was simply part of a dream. Then I gradually became aware of a very real dark presence.

Hisss.

I opened my eyes, a little fearful of what I might see. The very first gentle rays of morning light peeked into the cave. Cautiously, slowly, I turned my head in the direction of the ominous sound.

There, in the faint light, an enormous black crow leaned over Riola's head. With the tip of its beak right near her ear, it seemed to be whispering strange sounds as she slept. As my eyes grew accustomed to the light, I saw her face contort into a harrowed expression. Whatever the bird was "saying," it was obviously nasty. How long had it been there? I remembered the gigantic black bird that I had spotted the evening before. Could it have been the same one? Had we been followed?

Do something! Do something! I thought.

Fear had frozen my limbs. At a rough guess, the crow probably stood as tall as my waist. Yes, it was enormous, unlike any bird that I knew. In the end, I had to decide. I couldn't let the coward in me win - doing nothing felt too awful. And besides that, Riola was my only way out of Khülm. Even if my intentions were selfish, I knew I couldn't just sit back and let her get hurt. So, plucking up all of the courage I possessed, I jumped up and waved my hands.

"Get…get…a…away!"

My voice practically failed me. Little more than a whisper came out.

I hoped that, if worst came to worst, the trolls would come to my rescue.

The bird looked up in silence, fixing its glare on me.

"Get...get...a...a..."

I tried hopelessly to yell again.

To my horror, the creature lunged towards me in one enormous hop. Thrusting its head forward, it stretched out its neck and opened its huge wings to their full expanse.

"Oh no!" I gasped. "What have I got myself into?"

It all felt like a nightmare; I desperately wanted to run, but couldn't move a limb.

Strangely, Riola and the trolls slumbered on. I thought that they must have been in some sort of trance. Then I landed on the cave floor, and had no more time to think.

I thrashed my arms and legs about in a desperate attempt to avoid the enormous lunging beak. The bird still hadn't made a squawk, as if determined to carry out its attack in absolute silence. Perhaps it knew that waking the trolls would be a foolish move. So I mustered all of my breath, and let out the loudest yell I could manage.

Although I did make a noise, my cry for help did nothing. In fact, the bird pecked and scratched all the more furiously. It felt like being pulled through a thorn bush. Not one of my limbs escaped the fury of the hardened beak and claws. I realized my helpless defense had carried me deeper and deeper into the cavern, away from the sunlight and my companions. The bird was far more intelligent than I had thought possible, and I feared it would peck me to pieces in the depths of the cave.

A long, deafening bellow echoed out across the cavern. The bird paused and looked up. Thankful for the distraction, I seized the moment. I hauled myself off the sandy floor and darted for the light of the entrance. I nearly collided headlong with Humphrey charging furiously towards the crow. Bella and Mrs. P, looking startled, ran behind him. The tumult had finally awoken them. Humphrey, usually so shy, had transformed into a charging ball of rage. With tusks raised and hair on end, he confronted the crow, hauling the other two behind him. A curdled mix of bellows and squawks emerged from the back of the cave as the creatures battled it out.

I collapsed on the ground right next to Riola, exhausted. She sat bolt upright, looking very confused.

"What's going on, Cole? What on earth happened to you?"

Her eyes flitted between watching me nurse my wounds, and the momentous battle unfolding at the bottom of the cavern. I opened my mouth to explain, but she shouted, "Look out!"

We both sprawled across the floor as the great crow shot out of the cave at blinding speed, missing our heads by a mere inch. The cunning bird had been no match for three angry trolls, even with its abnormal size. Humphrey and his two friends came huffing and puffing from the depths a few minutes later. They looked completely wired, with their hair standing on end and their tiny black eyes glistening with energy.

"What happened?" asked Riola for the second time. "You look awful!"

I dragged my gaze away from the trolls and explained how I had seen the crow when I awoke. I also told her about the enormous black bird that I had seen in the branches of the tree the night before.

"Are you sure you haven't ever noticed that crow?" I asked. "It could've been keeping an eye on you."

"Never in my life, and I'm certain about that."

"Really? Never? That bird was huge, and it knew exactly where to find you. It was so focused, too, so determined, like it was delivering a message. And when it fought me, I could have sworn that it was intelligent."

"Why would it be interested in me? I'm a runaway slave girl, a nobody!"

"I'm not sure," I sighed. "The whole thing feels a little weird, that's all.

"Here," she said, handing me a bottle of ointment. "Put this on your wounds."

I rubbed the strange cream into my cuts and grazes, and it stung so badly that my eyes watered.

"Cole, did the crow actually use words? I mean; did the noises it made sound like a kind of language?"

"I couldn't say. I heard some muffled sounds and that's about it. I wasn't really close enough to hear. But the look on your face said it all—it obviously upset you."

"That doesn't sound too good," she replied. "Anyway, it's gone now, and I'm utterly exhausted." She slumped back under her blanket and fell asleep.

Riola's lack of concern unsettled me. I began to wonder if weird things were simply a part of her life—I had followed her into a different world after all. For me, on the other hand, the events of the night gripped my imagination. I lay awake, thinking, long after the others had fallen asleep. Clearly, the crow was no ordinary bird. Apart from its enormous size, it showed cunning. Riola had no problem with the possibility that it could use language, so it probably did. But why had it picked on her? If it was on a mission, then who could've sent it? Daylight steadily approached, and it must have been about five in the morning before I drifted off to sleep.

It didn't last long.

A short while later, a definite chill seeped into the cave. I curled up beneath my blanket, but the cold air worked its way into my bones. I could see the trolls shivering as they slept. Riola had also snuggled up into a tight ball, but she seemed otherwise unperturbed in her dreamland.

"Could it really be this cold?" I asked myself. "It's chillier now than it was in the middle of the night."

Exhaling gently, I noticed that my breath formed a little cloud. Something was definitely wrong—the rising sun should bring warmth.

About five minutes later, I noticed a very peculiar musty smell, followed by a faint, but definite sniffing sound. I sat bolt upright, trying to work out if my imagination was playing tricks on me. No, the sniffing sound got louder every minute. The strange musty odor had become almost unbearable.

Then I heard a steady shuffling noise, intermingled with the ominous scraping of clawed feet. The giant bird had blown away my unbelief in mythical beasts, so I prepared to encounter almost anything. The sound of the creature's approach grew louder by the second—I knew it must be close, though I couldn't work out which direction it was coming from. Myriads of tunnels opened up into the main cavern, making it impossible to tell which sounds were real and which were echoes.

I shook Riola, trying to wake her. She moaned in her sleep, and pushed down deeper under her blanket.

Snarl!

A deep growl came from somewhere in the darkness.

"Riola! Get up!" I pleaded.

The sleepy girl lifted her head, and mumbled with irritation. "What's the matter?"

"There's something in the cave!" I exclaimed.

Riola finally hauled herself up with a sigh, and rubbed her eyes. And then her entire body stiffened.

"Why didn't you wake me earlier?"

"I tried," I replied defensively. "It didn't work."

"We need to get out now!" she yelled. "The cold air, that foul musty smell—it could only be a Myurim!"

"A what?" I asked in confusion.

"Never mind." She sprang to her feet. "I'll get the trolls, you head for daylight!"

I looked over to Humphrey, expecting the leader to have woken up. No such luck; he lay coiled in a tight huddle on the floor, deep in the murmurs and twitches of a troll's heavy sleep.

"Get up!" yelled Riola, tugging on their chain.

ROAR!

I jumped with fright, and swung around to face the creature. I could still see nothing, but the air was thick with the foul, rancid stench. Straining my eyes, I peered into the darkness until I glimpsed something. A large shape moved toward us from one side of the cavern. The black beast lurched awkwardly, almost as if injured. As it came closer, I noticed that it held its head high, sniffing the air vigorously as it went.

"GET OUT!" screamed Riola.

"It's half blind," I replied. "Look at the way it's moving. Do you think it can even see us?"

"It doesn't need to see you," she yelled. "It can hear and smell you."

Curiosity seized me. There wasn't enough light to see details, and something inside me wanted a better look at the brute. But Riola grabbed my shirt and literally hauled me out of the cave. I saw the dark beast emerging, seconds before it let out another bellow—this time shaking the rock walls of the cave.

The almighty sound woke Humphrey and his companions. They lurched out of sleep, wearily facing their aggressor. The sound of clashing tusks and furious snarls resonated within the cavern. Even three against one, we had no idea who would win. Humphrey, Bella, and Mrs. P were almost unable to cope with the ferocity of the assault. At one point we heard a yelp, and Riola felt sure that Mrs. P had been wounded. I worried about whether we should help.

"Shouldn't I at least throw something at it?" I asked urgently. As the words left my mouth, Riola tore back to help her trolls. I reached out as she sped past, managing to seize her by the arm.

"You must be mad!" I yelled. "There's no way you can stop that creature. You told *me* to run!"

Suddenly, a direct shaft of sunlight pierced the cave entrance. The enormous brute let out an ear-piercing holler, and swung around to stagger off into the depths. As blind as it may have been, it was obviously very sensitive to light. Humphrey and Bella stood panting inside the cave mouth, and Mrs. P lay whimpering in the sand.

"Let me go," yelled Riola, pulling her arm free from my grasp. Inside the cave, she found her blanket, tore a strip from one of the frayed edges, and bolted across to where Mrs. P lay.

"Oh, you poor thing," she sighed. "What a horrid night! Cole, look in my bag for that small bottle of ointment. Please bring it here."

Still pulsing with adrenalin, I found the bottle and passed it to her. She smeared some of the cream over the strip of material and bandaged Mrs. P's leg.

"I don't think it's too bad," she said with relief. "We're lucky, any deeper and she would've been in real trouble."

"Poor Mrs. P," I replied, "and she fought so bravely. Tell me, what did you call that creature? I've never seen anything like it!"

"A Myurim, or dark troll," she answered. "They began life like Humphrey or Mrs. P, but then they were corrupted. That one probably woke up during the battle against the crow. The Myurim hate normal trolls—we're lucky Mrs P wasn't killed."

"That sounds awful. How were they corrupted?"

"There's no time to talk about that now. We need to get going. It's not safe here anymore and, when midday comes, the trolls will struggle with the sunlight."

Riola packed the blankets into one of the bags as she spoke, then swiftly tied the bag to Humphrey's back. She told me to sweep away our footprints with a branch; the less evidence we left, the better. In the meantime, the trolls snuck out to forage through the plants that grew around the mouth of the cave.

"Do we get to eat before we leave?" I asked.

"Well, if you can call it breakfast," she replied. "We're having dried legumes again. You're not going to find our meals quite as good as what you're probably used to."

When all was ready, we left the cave and headed out into the morning sun.

"It's already far too light," she cautioned. "We won't be able to travel very far. I was hoping to reach the Khülm Trading Ruins by lunch—now I think we'll only make it by nightfall.

"What are the trading ruins?" I asked.

"That's a big question."

I listened, fascinated, as Riola described how Khülm had fallen from beauty and prosperity into chaos and oppression after its neighbors to the west, the Morodians, mounted a ruthless invasion. The battles triggered a series of events that brought untold evil into the whole region.

—o◯o—

General Mershnin, the most valiant of the Morodian commanders, brought his horse to a halt. It was late afternoon, and the whisper of a gentle breeze cooled the warm, humid air. Another long winter had passed, and the summer rains were finally on their way.

A soft glow of sunlight danced over the landscape, washing the horizon in a peaceful haze of gold. In this tranquility, the general's armor glistened and his shield sparkled with the expectation of war. This man commanded the fear of his troops and enemies alike, a towering pillar of muscle with a will of iron and a temper to match. Before him lay Khülm and behind him stood row upon row of infantry. To his right, an expectant cavalry awaited orders. Every hand clasped the hilt of a sword, every horse champed at the bit. The mighty general raised his sword and yelled the long-awaited command.

"CHARGE!"

That day the beautiful land of Khülm was overrun, and her proud history came to a halt. For, as General Mershnin's troops poured into the main city and as his cavalry surrounded the Palace Grounds, the ruling Khülm dynasty argued about how they should respond.

They had known for three weeks that the Morodians would attack, yet they failed to prepare for the invasion. In truth, the people of Khülm were not fighters; they loved art, music, and literature. To them, the words *army* and *battle* described nuisances, concerns that merely got in the way of their love for life.

Looking back, their disinterest in defending themselves was unwise, for their neighbors, the Morodians, were a war-minded people who had desired the beautiful, fertile land of Khülm for many years.

During the invasion, a few brave members of the Khülm Royal Guard plucked up the courage to fight back. Their bravery was of little use; General Mershnin's soldiers dispatched them with ease. Before long, the inhabitants of Khülm lost all hope and fled.

One group of determined families stayed behind to fight for what little they had, led by Lord Khlorinn, a senior member of the

Khülm aristocracy. Full of grief, and desperate to save his collapsing culture, he sent a letter to the Truark tribes who lived beyond the western border, asking for their help. If they came to his aid, Lord Khlorinn promised them a share of the land. Unfortunately, this proved to be a very misguided decision.

The Truarks, a nomadic people, were infamous for being extremely wily. Although they would never have admitted it, they were bandits at heart. Their most powerful warlord—a great, big, burly man by the name of Drimmik, known for his enormous grin and razor-like teeth—was also the most cunning of all Truarks alive. To be fair, he did have a soft spot; he had a great affection for his family, as did most Truarks. I suppose you could say that he was a giant scoundrel with a well-hidden, warm heart. Driven by the desire for land, Drimmik answered Khülm's plea and, according to his character, he went about it in a very clever way.

Needless to say, the Morodian invasion succeeded and their forces occupied Khülm, although Lord Khlorinn and the Truarks continued their resistance. General Mershnin stayed in Khülm for quite a while. He set up his military headquarters in a deserted country manor and became obsessed with the desire to completely crush Lord Khlorinn and his Truark allies. His campaign continued until something, or someone, interrupted.

One morning, quite unexpectedly, a lovely young woman named Truwen arrived at his door. She offered her services as a chambermaid. If not for her beauty, she would've been turned away, but as it was, she became part of the general's staff that very hour.

Day after day, the persistent general went off with a group of soldiers to hunt for Lord Khlorinn and his cunning allies—he wanted to ensure that every single one was arrested. But, as time went by, things began to change. The mighty warrior seemed increasingly distracted from his duties by a growing love for Truwen. For the first time in his military career, the thought of battle bored him. Each evening he longed only to return to the manor. He fell deeper and deeper in love, unaware of his love's true identity.

After a few months, Truwen mustered the courage to confess

who she was—the daughter of Drimmik, sent to distract and spy on Mershnin. The general was shocked to the core, but, to his own surprise, he felt no rage. Compassion overcame him, and compassion was something that he hadn't experienced before.

Truwen had deceived him, for she had intended to beguile the leader of the Morodian army. That may be true, but, in the end, she fell for Mershnin as much as he fell for her. The general felt touched by her courage and honesty—and, of course, the fact that she loved him enough to tell the truth. Yet, for the first time in his career, he felt powerless.

Mershnin knew that he would never leave Truwen, he loved her too much for that; he had long since decided that he would ask for her hand in marriage. Nonetheless, what would he do when others discovered that she was the daughter of Drimmik? It would simply be a matter of time before his officers caught on, and then what? He could not return home; he would be arrested as a traitor. And the idea of waging war was unbearable. In the end, he took off into the night with his love, and together they sought a fresh start to life.

His army never quite recovered from the sudden loss of leadership, and the endless battle against the cunning Truarks began to wear them down. Eventually, the shamed Morodian governors admitted defeat, and pulled their troops out of Khülm once and for all. The wily Drimmik, though baffled, enjoyed the mesmerizing success of his plot. An entire army bent on his destruction had been thwarted by the power of beauty alone—at the sore price of losing his daughter. Sadly, the victory did not last.

Once the dust had settled, Lord Khlorinn and Drimmik did their very best to establish law and order—in vain. Various new Truark warlords rose up, each claiming a piece of land as their own and fighting over who should have what. Many turned against Lord Khlorinn, claiming that he would betray them, and the once respected aristocrat had to flee for his life. The Truarks lost what little unity they had and the chaos went from bad to worse.

Although still called Khülm, the country's soul had been torn out. Once Lord Khlorinn left, the last of the original families moved on. The elegant buildings of that great land fell into decay, and the well-built roads soon weathered and crumbled.

In the end, an evil opportunist from another land quietly and cunningly imposed his rule. Lord Grimmon skillfully encouraged the lawlessness, using it to his advantage. One by one, the Truark warlords fell under his spell, and a dark oppression spread its tentacles over Khülm.

These tragic events came to pass about sixty years before my journey with Riola through Khülm. If I had known more about them, I might have realized that fighting giant crows and dark trolls was merely the beginning of our adventure.

CHAPTER SIX:

Into the Fallen Land

══o◯o══

When we left the cave, Riola led us northwards along the edge of a towering mountain range. She kept up a good pace and, after about an hour's walk, we reached a beautiful archway that stood alone in the landscape. Constructed of small red bricks, it was flanked by a graceful pair of trees. We guessed that it was a relic of the days before Khülm was destroyed.

From this archway, a small flight of stairs led up to a simple landing and a road. The road climbed higher and higher until it became a pass that disappeared into the mountains. A gentle breeze wound its way down from the slopes.

"Oh perfect!" cried Riola. "I bet this leads to the Khülm Trading Ruins!"

"Great," I said with a smile. "That sounds good."

I had no idea why the ruins were important. Riola had chatted about the history of Khülm, but she hadn't said a word about where she was going. And, despite the tranquil scenery, little signs here and there warned us of the sinister world that lay beneath. The various symbols scrawled into the brickwork of the archway probably had been left there by Truark traders and bandits. Riola bent down and peered closely at the etchings, trying to decipher them.

"These aren't that old," she sighed. "We'll have to be careful from now on, or we may find ourselves being sold off as slaves."

"What do they say?" I asked.

"Not sure," she replied. "Truarks are known for leaving messages like this, but I can't work out what they mean."

I scanned the cliffs above and the dark line of trees that lay immediately to our left and right.

"Someone could be watching us right now," I whispered.

"I suppose they could," she replied. "We'll have to rely on the trolls; they're very good at sniffing out danger, and most thugs wouldn't take them on. Keep your eyes peeled though, anything could happen around here."

Her comment shot straight through me. On the first night we had battled two ruthless creatures. If that was only the beginning, what was to come? The more I thought about it, the more determined I became to fight my way back home.

"Riola," I exclaimed in frustration, "I want to know where you're headed!"

"OK, calm down. I'll tell you my plans this evening. First we must find somewhere to settle for the night."

"Why? Let's go back to the bridge right now. We can cross it together—it may be worth a try."

"No, Cole, we've already covered that option. I know you hate it here, but there are places worse than Khülm. What if we landed up in Goria? And, let's say we did make it back to Earth. Who says your parents would be there? We have no idea where Shyla took them. Anyway, it's not Earth I'm looking for."

"So what are you looking for?"

"Hmm…it's not what, it's who, and you'll soon see…hopefully."

"Huh, you're looking for a person? Who?"

"As I said, I'll explain everything tonight. It's a long story, and I'm not wasting time on it now. Be patient."

"Oh that's great! You're asking me to keep quiet and follow you. I don't even know if I can trust you."

"I'm not asking anything of you, Cole. Remember, you came looking for me. Leave if you want, but you won't get very far. Or, you could trust me, and I'll try to lead you to safety."

I turned around and looked back down the road. I wanted to run as fast as I could.

"Go on," said Riola. "I'm not stopping you."

She continued up the hill. I was trapped. Deep inside, I felt a black, empty space open up.

Why did you leave me Dad…Mum? Why?

How could you go without telling me?
I can't make it through this alone. It's a nightmare.

A part of me knew that Mum and Dad didn't just leave. How could they have stopped the serpent? I was so angry, so scared, but there was nothing I could do to make it all go away. Riola was right though, and she knew it. My only hope was to stay with her.

With the sun steadily rising, we forged our way up the ancient cobbled avenue. The further we went, the narrower it became. On top of that, the stones were wet and slippery. Mist and the chilly mountain air probably stopped things from drying out. I had to concentrate on every step, while trying not to look over the edge—the cliff to our right increased in depth as we climbed.

"Careful!"

I heard Riola's scream, then the pounding of an enormous boulder as it came crashing down from the slopes above. It tumbled right across our path before continuing over the edge of the cliff. We both dropped to the ground and covered our heads with our hands. Gravel and splinters of shattered rock landed all around us. For a few moments we stayed where we were, listening in horror to the resounding echoes of the boulder as it bounced its way into the valley beneath.

"That was close!" said Riola in a state of shock.

"Yes. Yes, it was," I replied, looking around. "It's a wonder none of us are hurt."

A little nervous, we finally got onto our feet and continued. As we had expected, it soon became too hot and too bright for the trolls. Riola suggested that we take a break. As it turned out, we came across somewhere to rest a few yards down the road. Considering where we were, we couldn't have hoped for more. A little path led off into a small, shady gorge that cut into the cliff. Spring water made its way down one of the cracks in the rock face—perfect for filling our bottles. So, on what little flat ground we could find, we curled up with the trolls and fell into a deep sleep.

Riola woke up first, annoyed that she'd forgotten about the time. It was late afternoon and a good resting spot like that off a well-worn trail wouldn't be safe for long. Riola woke me up first—I'd never been so tired in my life—and then Humphrey, Mrs P, and Bella, who snorted and grunted with irritation.

"Up you get!" she cried, pulling at their chain. "We need to reach the trading post by nightfall."

"Will it be safe there?" I asked.

"Probably not, but we'll be able to find a few supplies for the second half of the journey."

"Huh? What second half?"

"You heard me, Cole! When we reach the trading post we should be halfway—at least that's what I've heard."

"Tell me now will you. Where are we going? Who's this person you're looking for?"

"All right," she relented, "I'll tell you. It'll probably bring back a flood of memories I'd rather forget. First, let's pack the trolls and get back on the road."

We drank from the spring, filled our water bottles, and packed the bags. Once again, we shared some of the dry, bitter roots that had been our diet since the journey began. At times I wished I could join the trolls—they loved their meals. When everything was ready, we set off on the last leg of the day's journey.

The walk ahead was long and weary, much as it had been earlier in the day, but this time around we had a lot less energy. The cobbled road seemed endless, but the tenacity of the trolls surprised me; they kept on going no matter what. We had to keep our eyes peeled at all times, especially when we came across pockets of trees growing on the slopes above—the dense, shadowy places were perfect for an ambush.

I felt wary of more than our surroundings; Riola had fallen into one of her moods again. Being with her felt a bit like walking on eggshells. Very irritable, she hardly said a word. To be fair, I think she was worried about reaching halfway in the dark. However, after we had made some progress, she began to tell her tale.

"Cole," she said, finally breaking the silence, "have you ever heard of Father Bruëll? Some people call him 'The Ancient One'."

"No, I haven't—at least not yet."

"Really? Well, hopefully our journey will lead us to him."

"Oh. So who is this Father Bruëll?"

Riola threw her head back and laughed, her first boisterous laugh in a long while.

"Really, Cole," she teased, "didn't you go to school? Father Bruëll is probably the most powerful person known to these lands. Surely you've heard of him?"

"Nope. I don't think anyone else from my world has, unless I slept through that history lesson."

"Well," she continued, "the point is that he's the only one who can release the trolls from their chains. He's also the one person who can help me find Geltonia. And, if we're lucky, he may be able to tell you where your parents are. If he won't help us, no one else around here will!"

I breathed a sigh of relief. I believed what Riola said. She looked too hopeful and passionate to be telling a lie. I had no idea if we could actually find this man she spoke about, but at least there was hope.

"Where did you hear about him?" I asked. "How do you know where he lives?"

Riola's gaze drifted towards the horizon, her sullen expression returning.

"Hmm," she mumbled under her breath, "I heard about him when I was a slave in Gorr, in the mines."

"Oh," I said, surprised. "What a strange place to hear about a kind person like that."

"No more than a handful knew of him," she replied, "and it wasn't the type of thing you could speak about openly."

Before I had time to respond, she made a sudden gesture with her right hand and stood dead still. The trolls and I obediently stopped. The murmur of distant voices drifted down through the quiet mountain air. Evening and darkness were fast setting in.

"We must be near the trading ruins," she whispered. "When we arrive, don't look curious, whatever you do. And don't let anything take you by surprise!"

"Wonderful. Are you sure we're on the right road?"

"Well, this is the route I've heard about. I'm not aware of any others. Besides, we really need to buy some food; we can't live on dried roots for the rest of the journey."

I looked at the road ahead, trying to peer through the gathering darkness.

"This really isn't getting any better," I grumbled. "We're probably going from bad to worse."

"No, Cole, it will get better. How can it get any worse? Anyway, there'll probably be a hotchpotch of people at the trading ruins, including a few from the wasted Khülm villages, smugglers from distant lands, and others who'll be passing through—like you and me."

"Won't the trolls look a little out of place?" I asked.

"I hope not," she replied. "Trolls may not be common, but most people do know about them. They're in chains, too, which should make things easier for us. People will think we've been sent to sell them."

At that point, the trolls had given up waiting in silence and had meandered off to dig through a patch of undergrowth. Riola whistled gently, enough to catch Humphrey's attention. He and Mrs. P shuffled back, leaving the chain to drag Bella into line—she loved her food far too much and was always the last to stop eating.

We set off up the pass again, this time at a cautious pace. The thought of the market and better food sounded promising enough, but a part of me was really scared of what might be there. Still, I kept on going. Soon a haze of smoke filled the air. The higher we went, the thicker it became. My chest slowly tightened up and my eyes began to itch and water.

"Someone's probably burning coal," suggested Riola. "I bet they use fires to keep warm in this high mountain air."

A hunched figure suddenly emerged out of the darkness a few feet ahead of us. The poor soul, pushing a small but heavily laden cart, went by without so much as a murmur.

"We're really going to have to stay alert now," said Riola quietly. "None of us saw that coming."

Sure enough, hardly a minute passed before a second figure stumbled across our path. With a bent back, and much huffing and groaning, he struggled beneath the load strapped to his shoulders. We were obviously nearing the market, though it was almost impossible to see anything through the filthy night air. To our right, the gentle glow of a fire revealed a group of chattering women. They sat huddled about the flames, each grilling a strange assortment of foods. The sight of a cooked meal almost mesmerized me; I caught myself staring for a little too long.

"*Ho-tup wanimba!*"

I jumped back. The owner of the fire had seen my hungry eyes, and she wanted to make a sale.

"*Ho-tup wanimba!*"

I tried to hide behind Bella's enormous body. Too late! The women quickly realized that I was embarrassed, and a rowdy peal of laughter broke out.

"Don't make eye contact," whispered Riola, "and don't get too inquisitive! The fewer the people who notice us, the better."

A short distance on, the road opened up into a large cobbled amphitheater, surrounded by a low brick wall. Clusters of traders sat here and there, all preoccupied with organizing their goods. Even in the smoky air, the fires gave off enough light for us to see what was going on. I coughed and wheezed my way behind Riola, trying very hard to keep a lid on my curiosity.

An enormous tree grew at the far end of the amphitheater, with branches that reached up into the night sky. To the left of the tree, a flight of stairs led up to a second, larger trading area.

"We need to get up there!" exclaimed Riola. "That's where the stalls must be. I think this area is probably the forecourt, where the traders meet. If we want to find food and supplies, we're going to have to head over to the proper market."

At the sound of those words, my pulse quickened. I wasn't sure

I had the courage to go any deeper into the haze of smoke, chaos, and danger. Unfortunately, Riola gave me no time to decide. She set off with the trolls, their great chain grinding along as they went. We made our way across the cobbled forecourt and, strangely enough, no one paid us the slightest bit of attention—or so it seemed.

On the other side, in the branches of the tree beside the staircase, something caught my eye. I peered up into the leaves and saw a mass of tiny, pulsating lights.

"Look at those!" I exclaimed, my finger pointing high into the air.

"Put your hand down!" snapped Riola. "Those are only little insects—you see them everywhere in Khülm."

"They must be glowworms," I said in surprise. "I've never seen them in real life before."

"That's lovely, but keep it quiet," she warned once again. "We're trying to look like part of the crowd, remember?"

I gazed into the tree a little longer, and then my eyes came to rest on two enormous pythons. Something inside me shuddered. Was my imagination playing tricks on me? Yet, the harder I stared, the clearer they became. Two large, emerald green snakes lay perfectly still in the upper branches of the tree and, what's more, they stared back at me.

I froze, transfixed by the peculiar sight. Just then, a sharp jab in the ribs caught me off guard, and I swung around indignantly. Beside me stood a boy, about my own age and size, and brimming over with nervous energy. He glanced about cautiously and then drew close to my ear.

"Don't stare at the snakes!" he whispered, then darted off into the crowd. Before I could process that, Riola grabbed my arm and yanked me up the stairs.

"Come on," she snapped, "we need to keep moving!"

At the top of the steps, we found ourselves standing in front of a huge, bustling market, a labyrinth of brick towers, sweeping archways, cobbled squares, and winding alleys.

We had finally reached the ancient Khülm Trading Ruins.

All in all, it was a sad sight to behold. The once graceful architecture was badly weather-beaten, and the smoke of open fires had covered the brickwork in black grime. The sounds of incessant coughing, coarse laughter, and rowdy arguments filled the air.

Despite all its woes, the market obviously suffered no shortage of food and supplies. Traders claimed every single available corner, and anything imaginable was up for sale, from dried meats and fish, to clothes and battle armor. The air was ripe with a myriad of conflicting, pungent odors, some strangely attractive, some peculiar, and others simply horrid. There was no shortage of living things either. Stray cats darted about, hunting for an easy meal. Chickens scratched and clucked in rusty containers, eels squirmed within murky bottles, and parrots chattered endlessly from bamboo cages.

Riola led us to an inconspicuous stall and browsed her way through a display of cured meats, cheeses, and breads.

"We'll need to buy things that'll last," she said. "I don't have a lot of money, but hopefully it's enough for some wholesome food and a few more water bottles—I think we're going to need them."

"Shall I have a look around at the other stalls?" I asked.

"That probably wouldn't be wise," she replied. "We need to stay together. You do the watching, I'll do the bartering. Be on the alert for any sign of danger, and don't get distracted."

Her advice seemed wise enough, so I kept one eye on the trolls and the other on the surrounding market. Before long, I noticed a tall, dark figure standing motionless beneath the awning of a nearby stall. I didn't think anything of him, until I felt the peculiar sensation that we were being watched. In fact, I felt quite sure that the dubious individual had his eye on Humphrey, Bella, and Mrs. P.

"Someone's watching the trolls," I whispered into Riola's ear.

Although she took the caution seriously, the figure had disappeared before I could point him out.

"That isn't good," she whispered. "Trolls sometimes get caught and sold to the mines—they're useful for carrying heavy loads. Simple thieves wouldn't take us on, but larger, more sinister gangs would. We need to get across to the other side of the market and find a road out of here."

She paid for the food and water bottles, then packed it all into a bag.

"Now, let's get out of here!" she exclaimed.

As we swung around to leave, a deathly hush blanketed the area. Stall owners retreated into the shadows, and the chattering of customers ground to a halt. Within a few moments, the alleyway had cleared itself of all congestion.

"Something's wrong!" I whispered.

Riola merely nodded. Her eyes flickered about nervously. The trolls were too confused by all the smells to be of any help. Time stood still. And then, without warning, a large group of hefty men burst into the clearing. Really menacing, they were heavily armed with swords and clubs.

"*Hurrib em yamorn!*" the largest of the villains snarled. I had no idea what he was saying.

"They're Truarks," whispered Riola, "and they want the trolls!"

"*Hurrib em yamorn!*"

The leader yelled the command a second time and stepped forward to challenge us. With his sword raised and his eyes burning with aggression, he was obviously not open to negotiation. My courage failed completely, and I froze on the spot. The trolls had protected us in the cave, but now they had become the target.

"What shall we do?" I stammered in desperation.

"Run!" whispered Riola. "The trolls can be quicker than most people realize!"

And with one enormous heave, she yanked the chain that bound them, whistled a piercing note, and darted into an alleyway. The trolls recognized the urgency without hesitation, and took off behind her like a pack of charging bulls. My legs shot into action. Before I knew what had happened, we'd left the clearing far behind us.

Deeper and deeper into the market we pushed, crashing over booths and bursting through piles of merchandise. All the while, the shouting of the Truark thugs remained a few yards behind. We knew that, in a clear run, they would have caught us with ease, but the throbbing mass of people, coupled with the narrowness of the streets, kept them behind us. Yet our luck was running dry.

As you may remember, the market was built on the upper slopes of a mountain and Riola kept leading us higher and higher. The further she went, the fewer options we had. Finally, we dashed into a road that was no more than a muddy dead end, and the villains tore down on us with vengeance. Before I could gather my wits, I felt myself being hoisted into the air and roughly bound with a thick rope. I heard thumping, pushing, whining, and shoving as they surrounded and caught the trolls, skillfully avoiding their swinging tusks. Obviously the Truarks had captured trolls before.

Chapter Seven

Peering through a Barred Window

=○○○=

I couldn't tell you how long the whole chase lasted—at the time it seemed like a flash. After the humiliation of being captured and tied up, we were dumped into the grimy cellar of a castle. In one corner a small torch stood burning, while in the opposite wall, a tiny barred window let in a little fresh air. The confused trolls lay huddled together: Mrs. P whimpering, Bella gazing about blankly, and Humphrey seething in a quiet rage. Riola sat by the window, peering hopelessly into the darkness.

I had no idea what to think or say. Like the rest, I was covered in nasty bruises, gashes, and grimy blotches of mud. To make matters worse, the rope gnawed at my flesh. I itched all over, but couldn't scratch a thing. Flashes of the evening's events swirled through my mind, from the live eels that squirmed about in dirty bottles, to the huge brutes who had captured us. It had been a really awful day. And what would the morning bring? Would we be carted off to a slave market? A cold shudder went down my spine.

I should've stayed with Mum and Dad on the deck, I thought to myself. *Even if that wretched serpent did swallow me, at least I would've been with them! We'll never find Father Bruëll now. No one even knows we're here. We're completely alone.*

My home in Spain, laughing with friends, driving to the shops— these were all fresh memories. It felt so wrong, so twisted; I was there only a few days before. I covered my face with my hands, and fought back a flood of tears.

Eventually Riola broke the silence.

"Cole, I didn't really tell you much about the mine, did I?"

"No, not much," I replied, trying to wipe my eyes dry.

"It was horrid," she continued, "like living in a nightmare.

Of course, it wasn't just me; there were many slaves—some old, some young, and many from different lands. We were taught the Gorian language, so we could understand the guards."

Although I had guessed that Riola's life story would be tough, what she told me that night still shocked me. In fact, I was a little ashamed—my life had been so easy compared to hers. The most trying things I could remember were Dad's lectures about the stars or the importance of being *responsible*.

"Gorian is a very difficult language to learn," she said with a frown. "It has sounds that are impossible to get your tongue around, and many of the slaves failed miserably, no matter how hard they tried."

"What happened to them?" I asked without thinking.

Riola ignored the question and carried on; obviously, they would've been punished.

"A man by the name of Lord Grimmon rules over the Gorians. To most people, he seems normal enough; he's neat and charming, and he likes nice clothes. It's only once you get to know him that a ruthless tyrant starts to come out. And it gets worse than that..."

"Worse than being a tyrant?" I exclaimed. "What do you mean?"

"He would visit the mines from time to time," she answered quietly. "When he did, the slaves were forced to parade before him. On his arrival, absolute terror overcame everyone. I can still remember the hatred in his eyes as he glared over the mass of us, and he didn't blink at ordering an execution. At times like that he looked inhuman. I can't really explain it; he seemed to change into something else. It was as if another creature lived inside him, a creature that came out when the time was right."

Her voice trailed off; these were memories that she obviously wanted to forget.

"What work did they make you do?" I asked after a pause, unable to contain my curiosity.

"Well, I was good with animals," she replied, "and some of the slave masters saw this. Pretty soon, I was assigned to look after the trolls—they did all the heavy carting of the rocks and stones that had been dug up. That's when I first met Humphrey, Bella, and Mrs. P. Like the others, they were difficult to work with at times, but I had a soft spot for them. Those three were the most trustworthy creatures I knew and, considering the way we were treated, I figured that it would be good to have them on my side."

"And the Myurim?" I asked. "You never finished telling me how they came about."

"That all happened at the mines, too," explained Riola. "In the early days, the trolls would refuse to work. They used to rebel and go wild, and the guards were petrified of their strength. No one could control them properly. Lord Grimmon finally decided that some of the trolls needed to be made into guards. This was a very clever idea, because, at that time, only he could speak their language, if you can call it a language—they communicate with grunts and groans.

"Very carefully, he selected the ones that were bullies—those that had the most rage—and promised them lots of strength and power if they became his elite guards or *Myurim*. The foolish creatures fell for the lie. Sure, they soon grew to be enormous, almost invincible, but their minds were held captive and their hearts slowly died. They fell under the curse of becoming puppets to the evil will of a tyrant."

"Did it work?" I asked. "Did the Myurim bring order?"

"Yes, it worked all right," answered Riola. "Their might and brutality terrified the whole mine—no one dared to step out of line. Since the ordinary trolls were chained in groups of three from then on, there wasn't going to be another rebellion. Anyway, within a few years, the curse that had made the Myurim so powerful began to destroy them. Their muscles ached, their skin developed sores, and their eyes burned with pain. The little sight they had soon disappeared. I often heard them blundering about in the night, snarling and groaning. In time, bitterness and hatred completely consumed them, and they attacked the worker trolls for no reason."

"Didn't Lord Grimmon realize the problem? Didn't he do something?"

"Why would he have cared? He enjoyed seeing their pain and torment; the agony of others feeds his soul. And he knew that the mine would soon close down—we found less and less gold each day. He didn't care that the Myurim were dying; they weren't going to be needed much longer."

"*If* this Lord Grimmon is so fearful, how did you manage to escape with three of his worker trolls?"

"There's a story behind that. The mine eventually shut down, and Lord Grimmon did it in a spiteful way. The whole thing, including the rooms where the workers lived, was hidden miles beneath the surface—this made escaping almost impossible. One night a few of his soldiers arrived, and they simply closed and locked the gates to the entrance tunnel. Most of the workers and slaves were sound asleep, and so were the guards who should've been on duty. Not a soul knew what had happened. The following morning, there was mayhem. At first we thought that one of the Myurim had locked the gates out of revenge, but that turned out to be untrue. In the meantime, the guards fought a losing battle to keep order."

"Sounds like a nightmare!" I exclaimed. "How did you get out alive?"

"Well," she replied, "with the help of the Myurim, the guards did eventually bring about order—they were worried that Lord Grimmon would arrive and blame them for the chaos. By the second day, all of the reserve food had been eaten. To make things even worse, the oil for the lamps was running out; the mine was about to be plunged into darkness. It was clear that our plight was hopeless.

"By then, even the head guards were becoming suspicious. They feared Lord Grimmon, but they definitely didn't trust him. On the evening of the second day, a mob of slaves, guards, worker trolls, and Myurim all heaved against the massive gates. Eventually they burst open, and the entire lot of them ran for the hills."

"And that's when you, Humphrey, and the other two finally escaped," I said. "It must have felt incredible!"

"Actually, we left the mine a little later," she replied, "and I had a good reason for that. On the day of the escape, the worker trolls had been ordered to help with the great push against the doors. I was terrified that Lord Grimmon would return right then, with vengeance, so I did my best to protect Humphrey, Bella, and Mrs. P. I found the three of them, and we hid in one of the chambers until it looked safe to leave. It was midnight by then and, though empty, the mine was still chaotic. The place was a complete mess, and I only had one candle. It was terrifying."

Images of the Myurim filled my imagination. I could see them blundering into the open world, each enraged with an incurable hatred for life.

"Lord Grimmon obviously had his reasons for choosing not to return," continued Riola. "In the end, he probably couldn't have been bothered about a bunch of slaves and some hopeless trolls—we were worthless in his eyes. He may even have hoped that the Myurim would polish us off inside the mine. Either way, I don't really care. I'm free now!"

"Not really," I muttered quietly. "We're not exactly free."

"We are!" she snapped. "Compared to that mine, this cellar is freedom!"

Riola seemed to go somewhere far away. She stared out of the tiny window, her eyes glazed over, tears running down her face.

"Those mines were awful, Cole, absolutely awful. We were worked to the bone, punished for no reason, and underfed—to keep us weak. I knew that I wouldn't see my parents again, but I still ached for them every single day. Some say that homesickness passes; for me it grew stronger. Escape was a million miles away—I believed that I would die in that filthy hole beneath the ground."

Tears streamed down her face. She tried desperately to wipe them away with her bound hands—she hated showing any sign of weakness. I did my best to console her with words, but realized it was little use. In the end, we both fell asleep on the hard stone floor, and neither of us stirred until late the following morning.

The next day we were left to ourselves; either that, or we had been forgotten. Now and again we heard the ominous thudding of footsteps from somewhere up above. Each time we braced for the worst, but the worst never happened. We weren't hauled off to a slave market, and the trolls weren't taken away from us. For hour after hour we sat where we were, trying to keep warm and to fight off the panic that threatened to overwhelm us.

Luckily, the trolls had been bound with our bags still attached to them, so we could eat some of our food. The thugs who caught us had been in such a rush that they hadn't even bothered to remove our belongings—or maybe they guessed that a couple of raggedy kids wouldn't have anything of value. With our wrists and ankles still tied with rope, we shuffled over to Humphrey and opened one of the bags. Although we were starving, Riola suggested we eat as little as possible. Neither of us knew how long we'd be kept in the cellar, and our supplies were limited.

By evening time I began to think the worst.

"So…are we going to die in here?" I asked aloud.

"I doubt it," mumbled Riola. "There'd be no point in leaving us here. The trolls will make them a profit, and we probably will, too. Perhaps they're waiting for a buyer or something like that, who knows. One thing I can tell you, we won't be here forever, whatever the reason."

Right at that moment, a strange sound interrupted us.

Clink.
Scratch.
Scratch.
Clink.
"What was that?" I whispered in surprise.
Riola sat up and listened carefully.
Clink.
Scratch.
Scratch.
Clink.
"There it is again!" she exclaimed.

And then, to our surprise, the large steel-and-wood cellar door creaked open. I held my breath. Once again, the sound of my heart pounded right between my ears. *Is this it? Are we about to be dragged off to the slave market?*

I wasn't the only tense one; all three of the trolls had risen to their feet. Humphrey snarled, Mrs. P's ears twitched, and Bella sniffed the air intently.

To our relief, the door ground to a halt after opening a few inches. From the opposite side there came a long sigh, a huff, and then a great heave. The door creaked open a little further. And then, quite unexpectedly, a hushed voice called out.

"Excuse me? I'm going to need some help with this!"

The fearful mood within the cellar collapsed. Humphrey dropped his aggressive poise and leaned forward slightly, tilting his head in curiosity.

"Hey!" came the sound of the voice again. "Are you going to sit around in there, or get helping?"

"What do we do?" I whispered. "It could be a trick!"

"A trick? They wouldn't bother with games," replied Riola. "That's a kid's voice; I think it's OK."

"I hope you're right," I answered. "Either way, we're about to find out."

"OK, we're coming over," I said aloud.

I stumbled towards the door and took hold of the handle. I pulled as hard as I could, but very little happened—it's not easy getting a good grip with your hands bound at the wrists. To make matters worse, the hinges were badly rusted and the heavy door refused to give way. Then, with a sudden burst of determination, I summoned all of my strength and gave a hard tug. The door shifted.

"Shh!" came the voice from the other side. "Don't let it creak too loudly."

With a little more pulling and heaving, the door groaned and scraped until it was about two feet ajar. A lean boy stood before me, wearing grimy old clothes. He was probably about twelve or thirteen.

"Thank you!" he said with a smile.

He picked up the torch burning on the floor beside him and literally jumped into the cellar.

"Quick, help me close the door again," he said quietly. "You never know when someone may walk past, and I don't want to get caught."

Whoever the newcomer was, he had forgotten to introduce himself.

"Don't worry, I have the keys," he promptly continued. "We mustn't take too long; a little planning and then we're out of here."

And with that, he gave the door a good shove with his shoulder and it shut.

"Stupid things!" he exclaimed. "So easy to close, but so hard to open."

He swung around and drew a large knife from a scabbard on his belt. "So, whose ropes shall I cut first?"

No one said a word—the ease with which he handled the large blade made us feel very uncomfortable.

"My apologies," he said after a pause, "I haven't introduced myself. My name is Mirrakin."

"Mirrakin?" Riola looked astonished.

"Yes, Mirrakin," repeated the boy.

"I knew I recognized you!" she exclaimed. "You used to work in the same Gorian mine as I did."

"Ah," he replied, "you do look familiar. What's your name?"

"I'm Riola, and this is my friend, Cole."

"Cole," said Mirrakin with a smile. "That's a nice name."

Before I could say anything, Riola continued. "Aren't you the Truark boy who used to clean the kitchens?"

The proud spark left Mirrakin's eyes; his face crumpled into a forlorn expression.

"Not all Truarks are bad," he sighed. "OK, so maybe most are. I know we don't exactly have a good reputation."

"You certainly don't," replied Riola. "I could count the honest Truarks I've met on one hand."

"I'm not surprised," said Mirrakin. "Tell me, Cole, where are you from? Not these parts, right?"

"No, I'm not from these parts at all. I come from somewhere called Earth. It's another land, another world."

"Huh, where's that? I've never heard of it."

"It's miles away," said Riola, "but he's hoping to get back. The problem is, a water serpent took his Ma and Pa."

I glanced at Riola—I wasn't too sure I wanted her giving all of my secrets away to someone I didn't know.

"Wow, that sounds crazy," replied Mirrakin. "So you're kind of lost, Cole."

"Yes, I don't belong here. But I will get home. I will find my mum and dad."

Mirrakin stared at me for a while. His gaze was intense, a strange mixture of sympathy and doubt.

Then he changed the topic. "So, Riola, I see you've befriended some of the trolls. You were quite brave to take them with you."

"So what if I did?" she snapped. "I trusted these three the most, and I wanted to take care of them."

Mirrakin looked at the creatures with curiosity. Obviously, the young Truark was familiar with the beasts—he showed no sign of fear at all.

"Come on, Cole," he said, putting his torch down. "Let me cut those ropes for you."

"Oh great, and thanks for rescuing us!" I answered with relief. "How did you know we were here?"

"I saw you in the market," he replied as he turned to cut Riola free.

"Yes, I remember your face!" I exclaimed. "You're the one who warned me not to stare at the pythons."

"Well done. That was me, and I was also there when you were cornered by the gangsters in the alleyway."

At that last comment, all heads in the room turned toward him—even the trolls could feel the tension.

"So…you've been following us," said Riola in a suspicious tone.

"Not quite," he replied. "I spend a lot of time in that market. I know it like the back of my hand. I couldn't help noticing the two of you, so I followed you for a while."

"Why would anyone want to spend time in that rowdy place?"

I asked. "Do your mum and dad own a stall?"

"Uh, not exactly. I'm…I'm a slave of Lord Urratä, the owner of this castle." He hung his head, dejected.

"Hmm, Lord Urratä," mused Riola, "Lord Urratä…I think I've heard that name before."

"You probably have," mumbled Mirrakin. "He's infamous around these parts. I think he's in the service of Lord Grimmon."

"More than likely," she agreed. "How did you land here?"

"Like you, I was caught. After escaping from the mine, I made my way to these trading ruins. I needed to find work. Well, work I found—I just had no idea that I would be forced into it!"

"Why did you need to work?" I asked. "Couldn't you have gone back home?"

"Home? Home wasn't an option; it was here or nowhere."

"Wonderful," sighed Riola, "so now we're caught in the grip of another tyrant."

"Not exactly," whispered Mirrakin with a broad grin. "I've been planning to escape for some time now, and I think I've discovered how to get it right. We'll need to be swift, though—no time for dithering."

"How do we know you're on our side?" I queried.

"Because if one of the guards were to catch me now, I'd be locked up with you for a long, long time. And besides, I've cut you free from your ropes, haven't I?"

"Alright, fair enough," agreed Riola.

"As fair as you'll get," continued Mirrakin. "When I saw you in the market, I was buying food for the kitchens; that's one of my daily duties. You were obviously runaways, but I couldn't simply walk up to you and offer my help—those markets are crawling with Lord Urratä's spies. Not much happens around here without him knowing about it. Even the two pythons that Cole saw are in his service."

"I knew there was something horrid about those snakes!" I exclaimed. "They sent a shiver down my spine."

Mirrakin took his torch over to Mrs. P and inspected her chains.

I took the opportunity to ask Riola what we should do.

"Can we trust him?" I whispered.

"Well, his story seems to line up," she replied in a hushed voice, "and what have we got to lose? It can't really get any worse than this."

"Mirrakin," said Riola aloud, "I don't think you'll be able to unchain the trolls. You probably know this, but those shackles were forged deep in the Gorian mines; they're pretty much indestructible."

"Pity. These great big clanking irons will slow down our escape."

"And how do you hope to get us out of here?" she asked.

"This castle is built on one of the upper slopes of a large mountain," he answered.

"No kidding," interjected Riola. "We spent an entire day walking up a nasty pass on our way to the market."

"Well, then," continued Mirrakin, "you may have seen that the front overlooks the Khülm Trading Ruins, but there is an enormous forest at the back of the castle. There's no point trying to weave our way down the hill and through the market; we'd be caught. Our only hope is to make it to the forest, where we can hide. We must hurry, though; right now we have the cover of night on our side, and the guards will be changing shifts."

"That sounds all very good," said Riola, "although you still haven't explained how we get out of the castle."

"Well," answered Mirrakin, "this cellar is quite close to an outer wall. In that wall there's an ancient little gate, and it leads straight into the forest."

"A *little* gate," I said wearily. "Have you not noticed the size of Bella?"

"Ah," he replied, "she should make it through with a good push. Either way, we haven't got time; we must leave now."

He placed his torch beside the door.

"Right," he exclaimed, "we're ready to go! Cole, I'll need your help getting this open—please do it slowly; there can't be any loud creaks. And remember, keep an ear out for the guards!"

Eventually, and with considerable effort, we pulled the door open again. Despite working slowly and carefully, the hinges let out a great squeal. The pair of us froze on the spot. It wasn't a very good start with tensions already running high. Mirrakin and I cautiously stepped into the threshold and listened for any footsteps. We heard nothing other than a few bursts of laughter from the floors above.

"Perfect," whispered Mirrakin, "they're having a banquet. No one will bother to come down here; they don't stock any beer in these cellars. Now follow me, and be as quiet as you can."

For better or for worse, our great escape had begun.

We trailed behind Mirrakin up a short flight of stairs and into a passageway. The poor trolls, not quiet creatures at the best of times, clanked a lot. We ended up lifting their chain so that the links wouldn't clatter on the tiles. Luckily, we made it down the passage without attracting any attention.

Mirrakin guided us through an archway and down another short flight of stairs to a large, solid door, much like the one in the cellar.

"Wonderful," muttered Riola, "out of one dark basement and straight into another."

"Oh really?" teased Mirrakin with a sparkle in his eyes. "This door actually leads out of the castle; it's all about having the right key in this place."

He quietly opened the ancient lock and gave the door a shove.

"The problem here," he grumbled, "is that no one ever comes this way. These hinges don't get used; they're completely rusted."

He gave another determined push. With a squeak and a groan, the door opened. There we stood, breathing the brisk night air. As soon as we were all out, Mirrakin heaved the door closed again and locked it.

"Rule number one," he whispered, "always leave things the way you found them."

All was silent but for the call of a night bird that rang out from a nearby tree. In front of us was a garden, surrounded by an ancient brick wall. In days gone by, a loving gardener had tended the plants, but that age had long since passed. Vines and weeds choked the flowerbeds and the broken remnants of a statue lay scattered across the ground.

Mirrakin led us through the tangled foliage towards a wall on the far side. Once there, he located the small iron gate and fumbled in his pocket for another key.

"This is it," he whispered, "this is the gate I was telling you about."

"Oh great!" I exclaimed. "And...what if someone sees us escaping?"

"Then we make a dash for the forest. They won't follow us, you can be sure of that."

"Really? Why not?"

"A massive python lives in those trees. She sleeps during the day and hunts at night. She's even eaten a few of the Truark guards; they're petrified of going near that forest!"

"What did you say?" I replied with horror.

Bemused, Mirrakin looked at me. "We're all going to need a little grit to get through this. Stay focused and you'll be fine."

"Cole's had his fair share of nasty serpents," chuckled Riola. "He's not going to like your plan."

She was right. My nerves had taken one beating after another, and I felt like we were never more than a step away from the next threat.

"So...you're relying on a man-eating snake to protect us," I said after a pause. "Am I missing something?"

"Not at all!" he exclaimed. "She's our secret weapon—if we can get past her, freedom is ours."

"Huh? And what if we can't get past her?" I asked. "Surely we'd be as tasty as any of the guards."

"A reasonable point," agreed Mirrakin, "and that's where the trolls come in. As big as that python may be, she'd prove no match for them."

"How very shrewd," commented Riola. "I'd say you had the whole plan worked out when you saw us getting caught. You needed a little help to escape, and the trolls were it."

The young Truark never replied. With a cunning smile, he pushed his torch into the ground and opened the gate for us.

Riola crept out first. Mirrakin and I helped the trolls through the narrow opening, while she encouraged them from the other side. As expected, Bella, the last, was the hardest to get through. At first her enormous bulk wouldn't budge. We had to heave with all our might, edging her rear through the gateway inch by inch. As she was about to pop through, we heard a number of shouts echo from an upper window overlooking the garden. Mirrakin swung around and listened carefully.

"Someone's raised the alarm," he whispered. "They know we're missing; we'd better move it!"

At that very moment, a guard peered out of the window and scanned the garden. Both Mirrakin and I looked up, very nearly making eye contact with him—trying to hide was pointless. A series of shouts followed as he announced our whereabouts throughout the fortress.

"Hurry!" spluttered Mirrakin. "In a matter of seconds, a detachment will be in this garden!"

CHAPTER EIGHT:

The Giant Tree and the Silent Hunter

═══○○○═══

A burst of adrenalin rushed through our veins and, in one giant heave, we pushed Bella through the gate. Mirrakin grabbed the torch and the two of us bolted out of the garden. But before we ran into the forest, he locked the gate and broke the key off in it, using a large stone.

"They won't open that easily," he said. "We're going to need all the time we can get!"

Without losing another second, we made off into the trees. Moments later, the castle door swung open, and a group of guards poured into the garden, armed with spears, clubs, and torches.

The six of us tore into the forest as quickly as our legs would carry us. As soon as we had covered some ground, Mirrakin stopped briefly to stamp out the torch.

"We can't carry this anymore," he said while trying to catch his breath. "They'll spot us for sure! We'll have to rely on the moonlight from now on."

Even without the torch, we still had a good chance of being caught. To make matters worse, the trolls had left clear tracks through the undergrowth. However, thanks to Mirrakin's cunning trick of jamming the key in the lock, the soldiers hadn't opened the garden gate yet. In the end, they had to climb over the wall.

That's when the fun really began. As soon as they realized that they would have to chase us through the forest, a raucous argument broke out. We could hear it over our own footsteps and rasping breath.

"Shh, just stop and listen!" said Riola. "Can you hear that noise? They're actually fighting amongst themselves."

"What are they saying?" I asked, coming to a halt beside her.

"One of them must be a commander," she replied. "He's yelling at the rest to follow us; it sounds like most of them don't want to."

"Great," I said with relief, "then we've lost them."

"Not quite," she exclaimed, "I think a few are still coming!"

"Darn," sighed Mirrakin. "The higher ranking officers are always trying to prove how brave they are. And besides, they're scared to fail. Lord Urratä doesn't tolerate weakness very well."

"So…what's the plan?" asked Riola. "Didn't you say that the python would keep them away?"

"She already has," replied Mirrakin. "As you said, most of them have decided to stay put, except for those nasty officers. They'll probably group together and press on for a while—at least until the fear really kicks in. We need to get them to break up and search for us. Stalking about in ones and twos will make them prefect prey, and they know it."

"And how on earth do we arrange that?" I asked. "They'll be on to us soon enough."

"We climb a tree," replied Mirrakin. "When they realize that our tracks have come to an end, they'll presume that we've split up, and they'll probably do the same. And if they do see us in the branches, I seriously doubt they'll climb up after us. The python lives in the trees; she doesn't squirm about on the ground like a giant worm. Even those proud officers will want to keep their feet firmly on the ground."

"And trolls can climb trees?" I questioned with disbelief.

"They have a few times," affirmed Riola, "but not very high. They once climbed a fruit tree to get some very tasty blossoms. If I remember correctly, they cracked the trunk."

"That's good enough," replied Mirrakin. "They're not going to crack any of the massive trunks in this forest."

He wasted no time in choosing a suitably large tree with strong branches. Riola suggested that we get Humphrey to go up first, as Bella and Mrs. P would follow his lead. Showing Humphrey what to do was easy; Riola simply climbed the lower boughs of the tree and called him. It was a little harder getting him to respond quickly.

A first, he simply sat and watched, almost as if her antics were some kind of entertainment. That all changed when the officers began to close in on us—not even the trolls wanted to encounter a bunch of armed brutes. Humphrey and Bella heaved themselves up with all their might, with Mrs. P following.

While the trolls clambered higher and higher under the moonlight, Mirrakin and I brushed away our tracks with some fallen branches. Even with all the danger of being chased, there was a comical side to things. Humphrey and Bella huffed and puffed like small locomotives. Their muscles strained and their bones creaked so badly that Riola feared for their health. Mrs. P, on the other hand, was fairly agile, climbing her way up with surprising ease. The poor old tree moaned and groaned under the sheer strain.

We completed the maneuver in the nick of time. As Mirrakin and I clambered up the tree, the officers passed beneath us. I knew these soldiers were tough, but I wondered if they had forgotten how low their numbers were or how deep they had waded into the forbidden forest. I peered down and saw them talking quietly to each other. As Mirrakin guessed, they split up into a few groups of twos and threes. Clearly on edge, they glanced about with their torches blazing and their swords drawn.

The game was far from over, but somehow I felt safe high up in those enormous branches. I let myself relax, and gazed at the beauty that surrounded us. Apart from the awesome size of the trees, the entire forest was alive with glowworms. Almost every leaf in the upper boughs revealed a soft, pulsating light. It felt as if we had drifted into a sea of miniature, twinkling stars.

"Wow!" I whispered in awe.

"Amazing, isn't it?" said Mirrakin from a nearby branch.

"Yes," I replied. "Too bad this place is crawling with villains and thugs."

"*Myan wahad, myan wahad!*"

On the ground far beneath, pandemonium had broken out. The officers shouted to each other.

"Something has scared them," whispered Mirrakin.

"What is it?" I asked.

Before he could answer, another cry pierced the air.

"*Myan wahad! Yanör va-ur!*"

"This should be interesting," he explained. "One of them has spotted the python!"

"How...how big is that snake?" I asked nervously.

"Enormous!" he answered with a gleeful look in his eyes.

We looked down through the foliage and saw two of the officers a little way off. One pointed upward, waving his sword and shouting frantically. The other scanned the trees, a look of terror plastered across his face. And suddenly the guards did an about-face and bolted out of the forest. The python was definitely nearby.

Riola crept down from a slightly higher branch to join us. "Did you hear that? Sounds like our snake has arrived."

"It sure has," I replied, "and the soldiers have already fled."

"Like I promised," said Mirrakin with a smug grin.

"Lovely. What do we do now?" asked Riola. "Stay up here, or head for the ground?"

"I think we should stay put for a while," cautioned Mirrakin. "If we start climbing down, the python might be attracted by our movement."

"Ah, didn't you say the trolls would frighten her off?" I queried.

"They certainly should," he replied, "but we don't exactly want to invite trouble."

"Wonderful!" sneered Riola. "And how long do we stay up here? Has the clever plan left us stranded in the treetops?"

"Precisely," I said in agreement. "And if the python does attack, how on earth would the trolls protect us? I can't imagine them pouncing across the branches—they'd probably fall to their deaths."

"Oh, back off!" snapped Mirrakin. "Perhaps you'd both like to go back to that cellar, huh? There's no point in going over all of this now. Besides, we'll be fine if she's already eaten."

"And if she hasn't?" questioned Riola. "Are we supposed to wait patiently while she picks one of us out?"

As it was, no waiting was required.

Almost as soon as the words had left her mouth, the branches beneath us began to creak and sway. The enormous hunter broke into view, its muscular body slithering and coiling through the foliage. For all its weight, I found the python's grace and beauty strangely captivating. I froze, gazing in awe at the deep green, metallic scales with a single white stripe.

And then, to our horror, the snake sensed that it wasn't alone. The slithering body stopped dead. A massive, triangular head rose up level with our perch. The edges of its mouth parted slightly, and a black tongue flickered out, probing the air.

We all froze, the trolls included. The snake focused on me; my worst fears had come true. I clung to my branch, eye-to-eye with the formidable creature, its tongue a mere inch from my face. I could hardly breathe; my mind had all but blanked out.

I could only think, *Don't move. Don't move. Don't move.*

And then, as quickly as it had arrived, the snake lost interest. The head dropped back down and the endless tapering body carried on with its journey. I nearly fainted.

"Well done," said Riola reassuringly. "You survived."

Unable to reply, I sat quietly on my branch, watching the glow-worms and humming to myself.

"Cole, are you alright?" asked Mirrakin.

"I should never have crossed that silly bridge," I finally mumbled. "Why, why, why?"

"There's no point in brooding over the past," replied Riola. "Anyhow, as far as I see it, you'll be all the braver for having come here."

Mirrakin looked as if he was about to ask a question, but before he could, Riola got us back on track.

"We should probably get going," she instructed. "The trolls travel best at night, and we need to be out of this forest by morning."

She whistled gently to attract their attention.

The trolls had only climbed the tree in the first place because they were so scared of being caught. When it came to getting down, they suddenly realized how high they were and balked. True to form, nervous Mrs. P was the most difficult to coax. Every time she moved, the branch she clung to would sway. This petrified her, and she would freeze up again. Eventually, Riola had to lead Humphrey and Bella down regardless, leaving poor Mrs. P to be pulled by the chain.

With a lot of heaving, shoving, puffing, and panting, we eventually made it to the ground. The air was quiet, the moon was still shining bright and, most importantly, we saw no sign of the guards.

"And now," I asked Riola, "do you think we're halfway?"

"Definitely!" she replied enthusiastically. "The Trading Ruins were exactly where I hoped they would be."

"Halfway? Halfway to where?" asked Mirrakin.

"To Father Bruëll," answered Riola.

A look of surprise came over Mirrakin's face. "Oh," he replied, "I see. Has anyone ever found Father Bruëll?"

"They must have," said Riola firmly, unpacking some of the supplies.

"Come on," she continued, "we'll eat as we travel. This place won't be safe in the morning; Lord Urratä may well send his thugs to search for us at dawn."

"Mirrakin, will you come with us?" I asked.

"Hmm, not sure," he replied. "Perhaps for a while. If you're headed where I think you are, you'll need to make your way across the Misran Desert."

"I thought so," said Riola. "I've heard about the Misran; it's supposed to be a really barren place. Do you know how to get there?"

"I can get you there," replied the wily boy. "As for going *through* the desert—that's another matter altogether."

"Oh wonderful," muttered Riola. "You think we won't make it, right?"

"Well, I'm not saying it *can't* be done," he replied. "I just don't know anyone who has done it. If you're really sure you want to, there's a gorge not far from here that leads down to the desert sands. People don't travel that way, so you won't have to worry about villains."

"Thank you," replied Riola, "and yes, I am sure…very sure."

"You won't be joining us?" I asked a second time.

"Well," replied Mirrakin, "I'm not sure how I feel about…"

"Searching for Father Bruëll?" prompted Riola.

At that moment, something caught Mirrakin's eye, and he darted off to investigate. A minute or two later, he returned clutching a sword.

"A real Truark blade!" he announced, beaming with delight. "One of the soldiers must have dropped it. We may well need it, and it's not too big, which is perfect. Most are a lot larger than this—the handles are too big for my hands."

Tired as we were, we trudged on for another hour, and what a peculiar walk it was.

A few minutes after setting out, we stumbled upon a group of tall silhouettes standing in the path. In the light of the moon, the images weren't very clear. I didn't even realize what was ahead until we came within a few yards. A group of tall, slender, silent men with thin, morbid faces stood their ground, ever so still. They wore simple brown and red robes, and each held a long spear.

"The Nagara," whispered Mirrakin as we stopped. "They were once the guardians of the forest, the protectors of the animals and trees. Lord Urratä deceived them and they joined his side. Then they discovered that he usurped their authority and cursed them. Now they stand alone, angry and powerless."

"You didn't tell us about them," said Riola quietly, "and they don't look particularly peaceful. Will they let us pass?"

"Don't worry, they're harmless," he replied, "but try not to look at them. They may crowd around us and stare for a while. If they do, keep going—the trick is not to stop."

"Why don't we walk around them?" I asked.

"If we try and go to the left or the right, they will follow," replied Mirrakin. "To pass the Nagara, you have to go right through the center."

"Aren't they frightened of the python?" questioned Riola.

"If they're as powerless as you say, surely they fear it? Why are they out at night?"

"The python leaves them alone," he answered, "and they leave her alone. Don't ask me why, or how it works. Come, we have no time to lose; we must keep going."

Mirrakin steadily and determinedly made his way through the quiet gathering of Nagara. Like it or not, we followed. As he had warned, they stepped forward and glared down on us. Somehow, I ended up well behind the others, pushing my way through the tall, slender bodies and menacing spears all on my own. It was terrifying.

"Keep moving, eyes on the ground," I repeated to myself. "Don't look up, don't make eye contact, and don't stop."

When I had almost reached the center, one of the Nagara stood right in front of me, blocking my path. With my heart pounding, I pressed on and jostled around him, half expecting to feel the sharp stab of a spear in my back. No blade pierced me, and I was not physically harmed. However, as I pushed through, he bent down, grabbed my arm, and spoke something into my ear.

Ka mata atanum.

For a split second I froze, not knowing what to expect. I couldn't help but glance into his deeply set, dark eyes—they were more like holes than anything else. The Nagara tightened his grip and repeated the words. They sunk into my mind. Even though they were foreign, I couldn't forget them. They came with an ominous feeling. As quickly as it had happened, the warrior suddenly released my arm, and I hurried forward, desperate to get away.

When I had pushed my way through to the other side, I saw Riola, Mirrakin, and the three trolls waiting for me. They looked completely unperturbed—obviously they didn't see what happened.

"So, that wasn't too bad," said Mirrakin with a wink.

"Ah, one…one of them said s-something to me," I stammered.

"Oh, what was that?"

"Well, I can't quite pronounce it, but it was something like '*Ka mata atanum.*'"

"Really? He spoke in a Truark dialect. The words mean '*the one* *who has been abandone*d'. Don't let it bother you. The Nagara aren't pleasant, they're full of nonsense. Just ignore it, Cole."

Despite Mirrakin's advice, I couldn't simply let the whole thing go. The words resonated too deep to be forgotten. And, why did the horrid warrior choose me? *Keep yourself together*, I thought to myself. *Just focus on finding Mum and Dad. I will get out of this mess. I will.*

As we walked on, the landscape changed. The density of the forest increased with every step we took, yet the trees themselves got smaller and smaller. The undergrowth became a thick, unruly carpet, almost impossible to get through. Mirrakin hacked away at it with his sword and managed to clear a path for the trolls. Nevertheless, the effort wore him down terribly.

After a while, Riola and I began to wonder if he was lost.

"Have you ever been here before?" I asked.

"Yes, I have," he replied firmly. "You must remember, I wasn't leading two others and a group of trolls at the time, and it wasn't the dead of night, either. It was a long time ago, when I was taken on a hunt by the guards."

"So people do come out this way!" I exclaimed. "Earlier you said they didn't."

"Well, perhaps they do…from time to time," he replied. "It wouldn't be at night, though—they'd want to avoid the python."

"How much further to the gorge?" asked Riola.

"Not too far," replied Mirrakin, "but let me warn you now, the route becomes harder to follow, even in daylight."

Despite all the difficulties, he did manage to take us the right way. Before too long, the ground descended sharply. We were obviously approaching the mouth of the gorge. The forest had been reduced to a matted growth of gnarled, thorny shrubs and entangled vines. The further we descended, the more Mirrakin used the sword to clear a path. And of course, the trolls were very uncomfortable; their great chain got caught in the foliage every few yards.

As the gorge opened up, however, the knotted undergrowth gave way to boulders, ferns, and the odd clump of trees. We descended until we arrived at a deep, still pool that lay between large rocks. From there, a stream flowed down the rest of the gorge until it disappeared into the Misran. There was just enough room to rest, eat, and wash our faces beside the pool. We knew that we'd have to find a larger place to settle for the night, but we needed the break—I was absolutely exhausted.

Before we moved on, Mirrakin called Riola and I aside.

"Come," he said, "I want to show you something."

He picked his way between the boulders, following a faintly visible trail that led away from the pool. After a few yards, he pushed through some branches that had fallen across the path and we clambered after him. On the other side, we found ourselves standing on a gigantic boulder that protruded over the edge of a cliff. Beneath and beyond us, the world fell away into a colossal, flat valley that stretched out into the horizon. The sky was also vast, a fantastic dome of flickering stars.

"Behold, the Misran!" declared Mirrakin. "Here, the Khülm plateau comes to an end, marked from east to west by one long cliff, as far as the eye can see. To the north, there's sand, sand, and more sand. The gorge we are going down is the only way to reach the desert."

"You've been here before," accused Riola. "And right on this spot, too."

"I have," confessed Mirrakin.

"So," I queried, "was that on the hunt?"

"Not exactly. I promised myself that I would get out of the castle, and those nasty trading ruins, once and for all. When they took me on the hunt, I memorized the route that the guards used. After that, I just had to wait for the right time to escape."

"And what happened?" probed Riola with rising curiosity.

"Well, I overheard conversations about the giant python," continued Mirrakin, "and I realized that I would have to make a run for it during the day. That made the whole thing very risky. Anyway, a few weeks later, I picked my moment and headed for the Misran as fast as I could. But…" He trailed off.

"But what?" asked Riola. "You can't stop there!"

"Someone spotted me leaving," he sighed. "I made it all the way here before a small detachment of guards caught up."

"That's too bad," I said. "At least you had the courage to try. What did they do to you?"

"They locked me up for ages," he answered. "And they've kept a close eye on me ever since."

"Oh wonderful!" exclaimed Riola. "So if they want us, they know where to find us."

"*You're* the ones who needed to be taken to the Misran," he replied. "And, like I said, this is the only route. If they do come after us, they'll probably leave in the morning, when the python is asleep. We have plenty of time."

"You *were* headed for Father Bruëll," I said after a pause. "You do know about him."

Mirrakin hung his head and then abruptly changed the topic.

"At least I know what they hunt out here," he said with a sparkle in his eyes. "The most beautiful deer live in this area. I caught sight of one, which is really lucky—they're extremely shy."

"Whatever!" snapped Riola. "You say what suits you at the time. How safe is this gorge if hunters come here?"

"Oh come on!" replied Mirrakin. "This is Khülm; nowhere is safe."

My mind wandered. I stood staring at the horizon, trying to guess the size of the desert.

"Mirrakin, how far is it to the other side of the Misran?" I eventually asked.

"You'll be travelling northwards," he answered, "which isn't that bad—perhaps two solid days of walking. Although the Misran is very long, it's not very wide."

"Two days sounds do-able," I said with relief. "But, then, why don't more people cross it?"

"Good point," he replied in a whisper. "You see, it's not all that easy to reach the other side without…"

Mirrakin looked about with an uneasy expression.

"Not easy to reach the other side without what?" I asked in frustration.

"There's an old rumor," said Riola, "that Lord Grimmon guards the far side of the Misran; he won't let anyone out of his domain."

"He won't let anyone out!" I repeated with alarm.

"Yes, that's exactly what I was trying to say," affirmed Mirrakin. "And as I said, I've never met anyone who did make it across. Then again, I don't know anyone who's tried in the first place."

"Why does Lord Grimmon care about a barren strip of desert?" I asked. "And anyway, would he really bother about some kids?"

"No, not usually," replied Mirrakin. "You see, the issue isn't actually the desert, or even who you are. It's what's on the other side of the desert that's important."

"Exactly!" exclaimed Riola. "Lord Grimmon hates people; he controls, imprisons and finally destroys them. We're trying to get to Father Bruëll, to escape, to find freedom. Lord Grimmon has a very deep, personal hatred for Father Bruëll. That's the problem. He'll try and stop us every step of the way.

"And the lands beyond the Misran belong to Father Bruëll?" I queried.

"You've got it. There's a huge battle going on—a battle between two kingdoms."

"And we're about to get caught up in it, right?"

"Yep," sighed Mirrakin, "and if you make it to the other side, you'll see how much of a battle it is."

Once again my hopes were dashed, and I felt powerless. The beauty of the enormous sky and endless horizon disappeared. I remembered Dad's astronomy lecture from our last night together. A wave of sadness and fear passed over me. "How could you leave me here?" I whispered under my breath. "*I won't survive a trek across a desert, or an attack by Lord Grimmon. I'll never make it home.*"

Chapter Nine

No More than a Slave
═══o○o═══

We made our way back through the foliage to the pool, where the three weary trolls lay in a huddle. They had fallen asleep, and the rhythmic drone of their breathing gently reverberated through the air. Riola woke them up and coaxed them onto their feet.

"Why don't we camp here?" I asked. "I'm exhausted."

"If it rains tonight, we'll get soaked," replied Riola. "Besides, there may be enough room for one person and the trolls, but not for all of us."

So, guided by the light of the moon and Mirrakin's keen eyes, we followed the stream a little further down the gorge. It was no easy task. Dark shadows lay between the boulders, and the rock surfaces stayed slick—all the right ingredients for a nasty fall. As usual, the chain that bound the trolls kept getting caught or locked in twisted positions. Mirrakin and I worked double-time to clear the way, but Bella still needed a whole lot of encouragement—she kept falling into a heap and grumbling.

After a little while, we stopped at the edge of a large boulder. The stream disappeared over the top of the great stone and became a tall, elegant waterfall. About fifteen feet beneath that, the water plummeted into a clear pool. On one side of the pool, a sheer rock face towered up into the night sky. A knotted tree grew out of the side of the cliff and rose up into the gorge, filling the air with its sprawling branches. On the other side of the pool was a large, flat rocky base—perfect for camping.

"That's it!" exclaimed Mirrakin. "That's the place to settle for the night."

"It won't be easy getting down there," sighed Riola.

"Who said it would be easy?" he replied. "Do you see another option with enough room for all of us?"

So down we went, the decline becoming worse with each step—I couldn't believe that we were attempting it at night. Yes, we had the moon, but it was hardly enough. On top of that, I had sore feet, tired legs, and a million and one scratches, bruises, and cuts—I didn't know what had hit me. Riola seemed tired, too. She acted a lot more sullen than usual and was unsteady on her feet.

Carefully and slowly, we made our way down to the large, flat rock. It was wider than we expected, perfect for laying out our blankets and bags. The water from the pool was crystal clear, and the towering branches of the tree would shelter us if it happened to rain. Mirrakin guessed that we were about two thirds of the way down the gorge. It would be a short walk to the desert the following morning.

"Mirrakin, where do we rest once we're in the Misran?" asked Riola. "There'll be no pool or shade in that wasteland."

"You never know," he replied. "There's a rumor of an oasis—you'd better hope it's true."

"Hmm," pondered Riola aloud. "That doesn't sound too promising."

"You have to take the risk," he replied. "Stay captive, or go out on a limb."

Whilst they were talking, I wandered off towards the pool. A few gentle rays of moonlight passed through the trees, dancing and shimmering on the surface of the water. I noticed a slight ripple on the far side of the pool and stepped back, a little wary of what it might mean. It turned out to be a small, peaceful snake, gliding from one edge to another. I looked past it, at the waterfall and the huge pile of boulders next to it. We must have climbed down them to reach the pool. Was there a labyrinth of hidden tunnels between those enormous rocks?

"Anything could be lurking in there," I muttered. I scanned the area more carefully, keeping an eye out for anything suspicious. Behind the waterfall I saw a large opening. Did the waters of the pool run deep into that mouth, reaching far back into the earth? All of a sudden I felt very unsafe.

"Hey," Riola called, "you over there! Going to join us?"

"Yes, of course," I replied. "Say, would any dangerous animals come out this far?"

"Who knows?" she answered. "Trolls don't usually head for deserts. As for other creatures—well, as Mirrakin says, nowhere is safe in Khülm."

"Perhaps we should leave a fire burning while we sleep," I suggested. "It might be wise. You know; creatures of the dark don't like light."

To my surprise, Mirrakin agreed. "That's not a bad idea," he said. "Let's collect some wood."

Armed with our lanterns, he and I browsed about in the surrounding foliage. We collected a reasonable pile of dead branches, as well as some logs from a fallen tree.

"The large pieces are great," he said. "We can put them in last and let them burn slowly. We'll also leave a few branches beside the fire. That way, anyone who wakes up during the night can feed it."

The trolls had taken to shuffling about in the undergrowth, smelling every hole and crevice for edible plant life. This foraging came to an abrupt end once we lit the fire; the poor exhausted creatures wasted no time in settling down. We laid out our blankets and I fell into a deep sleep.

In the early hours of morning, while it was still dark, a sour, sickly smell woke me. I kept absolutely still and tried to focus my attention. The last time I had smelled such a bad odor it had been one of the Myurim. To my surprise, it didn't last long this time. After a few intense minutes it faded completely, and I breathed a deep sigh of relief.

Perhaps it was all part of a crazy dream, I thought to myself. I wasn't taking any chances, though, so I threw a few more logs onto the fire. With the flames crackling back into life, I went to sleep with my mind at ease.

My blissful rest didn't last long.

An hour or so later the smell returned, once again dragging me out of my dreams. This time the rancid odor grew stronger by the minute, with no sign of fading. When I could stand it no longer, I lifted my head and peered in the direction of the boulders. Thankfully the fire was still ablaze, and the leaping flames threw splashes of orange and yellow across the gorge.

I focused my attention on the openings between the boulders, but couldn't see anything unusual. Then I remembered the cave that lay behind the waterfall. There, to the right of the tumbling water, a large shape appeared to be rising out of the pool. It approached slowly, steadily, and very quietly. Soon the creature's entire form had emerged from the water. For a few minutes it stood in the shallows of the pool. To my horror, I saw it was an enormous Myurim, all dripping wet and sniffing the air.

I was transfixed, mesmerized. In the dancing firelight, all I could do was sit and stare. Two large, battle-hardened tusks protruded from one side of the massive animal's mouth, and a single bent tusk protruded from the other. Strings of thick saliva dripped and drooled from its lower jaw. It grunted quietly and ground its teeth. Twitching this way and that, its snout seemed eager to pick up a scent. The eyes were tiny little black beads, completely dull and useless for sight. Cuts and bruises mottled every inch of its body, the open wounds weeping, unable to heal. Almost all of its hair had fallen out, and its hands, fingers, and nails were bent, buckled, and twisted. There was so much agony about the wretched creature that it was almost painful to watch.

ROAR!

The gorge reverberated with the deafening sound of the Myurim's warning cry. I snapped out of my trance, and scrambled to my feet. I tried to yell, but an almighty smack knocked me to the ground. It had discovered the scent it wanted and had broken into a full charge, knocking me flat as it thundered past. With the air knocked out of my lungs, I could only watch in the flickering light as the enraged animal tore towards Riola.

The roar had woken Mirrakin. Always alert, he hauled Riola out of the way in the nick of time, literally saving her from the jaws of death. The Myurim threw itself at the spot where she had been sleeping, snarling in rage and thrashing its great tusks about in a wild frenzy.

"The sword, grab the sword!" yelled Mirrakin hysterically.

Dazed and still gasping for breath, I blundered about, trying to find the blade. I found it right near the spot where I had been sleeping. Taking hold of it, I staggered over to Mirrakin.

"Don't just stand there!" he yelled. "Stab it! Stab it!"

Desperately trying to protect Riola, he had resorted to pelting the Myurim with rocks.

Humphrey, Bella, and Mrs. P were awake now. Humphrey recognized the danger first, and strained against his chains to join the battle. Sensing the presence of the waking trolls, the Myurim made a final, violent lurch towards Riola. Quick as a flash, Mirrakin grabbed the sword from my fumbling hands and thrust it with all his might into the creature's flesh. He didn't stop there, either; he pulled the sword out and thrust it in again and again and again… The nasty brute roared with alarm and stumbled backward.

Bella and Mrs. P were fully alert by now, and Humphrey led the charge with a full-throated bellow that echoed up the gorge. For a moment it was all tusks clashing, dirt flying, and angry growling as the creatures battled it out. Mirrakin buzzed about the edges, stabbing wherever he could. In the end, the Myurim couldn't cope with three enraged trolls and a tenacious young Truark. The great beast tore away from the skirmish, winced, and then retreated to the other side of the pool.

Mirrakin set off in hot pursuit, determined not to let the creature escape. The trolls and I followed as fast as possible. We surged across the edge of the pool, between some boulders, and then through a thicket that lay downstream. The pursuit required a tremendous burst of energy, and the chain binding Riola's trolls uprooted plants as we went. Mirrakin was a few steps ahead, wielding his sword and jabbing at the Myurim with all his might. The final flurry didn't last too long—the brute ended up cornered right on the verge of a precipice. Snorting with shock and fury, it stumbled backwards over the edge of the Khülm plateau and disappeared into the darkness.

"That's the end of him!" said Mirrakin, collapsing on the ground to rest. The sword fell from his hand and landed with a clatter on the ground.

Still reeling from the shock of it all, I stood panting beside him. Mirrakin's display of bravery awed me. I felt energized by the victory, yet, at the same time, disheartened by my own lack of courage. Apart from my fumbled attempt to pass him the sword, I had been nothing more than a spare part. The trolls had made their valiant contribution—even the quiet Mrs. P had been transformed into a determined fighter.

"I'm going to check on Riola," I mumbled after a pause.

"Good idea. I'll clean up the sword," answered Mirrakin. "We'll need to keep it close at hand from now on."

"In fact," he continued, "you'd better keep it."

"Me? Why should I be the one to carry it?"

"Cole, you're going to have to fight at some point. The time will come when you'll have to defend Riola, and there are much worse creatures out there than the Myurim."

"Oh, wonderful—that's a bit hopeless!"

"Perhaps, perhaps not. Either way, I hope you realize that this was only the beginning of your battles."

"My battles? I'm not the runaway slave here; I don't even belong in this horrid place!"

"Really? Is that what you think? Tell me, do you remember the stories about Lord Grimmon?"

Mirrakin's calm, confident voice made me feel all the more unsettled.

"Yes," I replied, "I do remember."

"Well, that menacing tyrant is real," he continued, "and he controls these lands in a very nasty way. Even though Khülm may look like a mess—and it is—don't think he's not watching. No one arrives here without him knowing, and no one leaves without him knowing, either. He may let you wander into the Misran, but, like we said, when you try to pass into the lands of Father Bruëll, he'll send someone or something to stop you. You're one of his slaves,

Cole, like Riola and me. And, as the saying goes, 'Once a slave of Lord Grimmon, always a slave of Lord Grimmon.'"

"So how does he know I'm here?" I asked in protest. "Anyway, they were after the trolls in the market, not us!"

"Forget the market," replied Mirrakin. "He knew about you the instant you entered Khülm."

"He knew when I arrived? Explain that to me."

"When you first put your foot in this land, one of his spies was there, I guarantee you. It could've been a bird, a troll, or even a bandit; many serve Lord Grimmon in secret."

"Oh, no, the giant crow in the trees! It saw me the first evening I entered the forest."

"You were probably reported then, and I bet they've been keeping an eye on you ever since. Let's not forget the two pythons at the trading ruins. Welcome to the club!"

"If I remember things right," he continued, "your parents are missing, and you may never find them again. The chances are slim. You're more like us than you realize. You're an orphan and a prisoner of Khülm—little more than a slave really."

I slumped to the ground, unable to respond. In one sense, Mirrakin had told me what I already knew. I couldn't say for sure that I would find my parents. Maybe I was an orphan? Maybe I was a slave?

"Riola says Father Bruëll will help," I said quietly. "She told me…"

"Oh come on," interrupted Mirrakin. "Do you really think he'd help you? Who are you to a powerful person like that?"

"Well, if you believe that our journey is pointless, why have you been fighting for us?" I asked. "Why would *you* even try to escape?"

"I never said the journey is pointless, I just told you what you're up against. And sure, I've thought about trying to find Father Bruëll, even though I have my doubts about him. But, that doesn't mean I won't help Riola to escape from Khülm. The poor girl is so determined, how could I not help?"

"So you'll come with us across the Misran?"

"I'm not sure. I'll see how I feel about it later." He rose to his feet.

"Come on, Cole. Let's go and see how Riola is doing. Bring the sword with you."

Mirrakin whistled for the trolls as he stumbled back down the pathway. The three creatures, who had been sitting in a breathless heap, hobbled to their feet and followed obediently.

"Thank goodness for them!" I exclaimed under my breath. "We'd be dead without those trolls."

When we got back to the camp, Riola was trying to bandage her right foot. She glanced up as we approached.

"That horrid beast gashed my foot," she groaned. "How am I going to make it across the Misran now?"

"How bad is it?" asked Mirrakin.

"Bad enough. It's throbbing like mad," she replied. "I can't even walk properly."

She peeled back the bandages to reveal the wound.

"Ouch!" exclaimed Mirrakin. "That's pretty deep, but I suppose you're lucky it didn't hit something vital. At least you're alive."

"Thanks for pointing that out," answered Riola abruptly. A forlorn expression passed over her face. "When will all of this end?" she asked quietly. "When will it end?"

"You need to get some rest," advised Mirrakin. "We're all much too tired."

He tightened up her bandages and helped her climb under a blanket. The poor girl fell asleep as soon as her head hit the ground.

"Will she be OK?" I asked. "She seems so down."

"That wound will need time to heal; it's nasty," replied Mirrakin. "Tomorrow won't be an easy journey."

"Perhaps we should rest here a few more days," I suggested.

"That might be wise," he replied. "I don't think she'll agree to it, though. She'll want to keep moving."

Mirrakin placed a large log on the fire and settled down under his blanket.

He and Riola fell asleep almost immediately. I stayed awake for quite some time. Subtle noises kept me on edge, like a light crunch here or a gentle crackling of leaves there. My imagination ran away with me. Was that a footstep, or perhaps the slithering of a snake? I couldn't believe how quickly the others had drifted off, especially considering the circumstances.

A host of unsettling questions plagued my mind. *Was I the only one who feared another attack? Who would look after the fire if we all fell asleep? What if the soldiers decided to come after us again that night, despite the snake?* Quite apart from my swirling thoughts, the more I tried to settle down, the more I realized how battered I was. Every inch of my body had an ache, an itch, or a throbbing bruise. Apart from my recent injuries, some of the nasty scratches inflicted by the crow were still sore.

And, on top of all this pain, I felt hot, sweaty, irritable, and in serious need of a bath. Once or twice, I even contemplated getting into the pool for a quick splash, but I knew I'd wake the others or attract another creature. So there I lay, rolling this way and that, scratching here, rubbing there, and trying to get comfortable on the hard rocky surface. During this restless time, I became aware of a whisper in the dark. I stopped my fidgeting and focused my attention on the voice.

I felt sure I heard the words "abandoned" and "worthless" being repeated again and again. However, before I could find the strength to investigate, my tiredness finally overwhelmed me. I fell asleep.

CHAPTER TEN:

The Faint Smell of Ginger

=○○○=

It was late morning when I finally awoke. Feeling dazed and a little confused, I sat up and noticed that the sun was already high in the sky.

"How on earth did we sleep so long?" I wondered.

I stumbled to my feet and scanned our surroundings. There didn't seem to be anything dangerous about. I had a good stretch and tried to ignore the fact that every muscle hurt and every joint groaned as I moved. I hobbled over to Riola, still soundly asleep. A few feet away, huddled at the base of a tree, the trolls lay in a blissful pile of snores and groans. I sighed and shook my head. You couldn't rely on a troll to wake you up. They loved sleep as much as they loved food.

I looked over to where Mirrakin had placed his blanket the night before. There was no trace of him. Why hadn't he woken us?

I wondered if he had got up early to scout out the route ahead.

"Mirrakin?" I called aloud.

There was no answer, so I called again.

"Mirrakin!"

Still no reply. Slowly, the sad possibility dawned on me. He had decided to go his own way after all. He had woken up while we slept and set off before we could talk him out of it. I knew he didn't think we would make it across the Misran, and I knew he had his doubts about Father Bruëll. Nonetheless, I still felt shocked that he had left, that we would have to go on without him. Was I really going to have to learn to use the sword?

I found his blanket neatly folded, with a piece of paper on top, held in place by a smooth pebble. He'd used charcoal to scrawl a message on the paper. I read the words aloud.

Everything will work out fine, my friends.
Go carefully and steadily.
And Cole, don't be afraid to fight; use your courage!
I need to follow my own heart from here on.
I hope I see you soon.
Take care,
Mirrakin.

I read the note again, slowly. As the message sank in, I felt anxious, uneasy, and unsafe.

"It's true, then," I mumbled. "He's actually gone. He's left us."

I glanced across to where Riola lay, still asleep. In addition to her injury, she had been growing more and more weary with each day. The mysterious girl that I met under the bridge seemed faded.

Hoping to shrug off my despair, I wandered across to the pool and gazed into the sparkling water. The rhythmic sound of the waterfall almost lulled me to sleep again. In that very place, the ominous Myurim had launched its vicious attack. In the light of day, the scene was transformed, the air clean and quiet, the sun's rays flickering on the shimmering leaves and the glistening boulders.

"Good morning!"

I swung around to see Riola standing a few feet away. Although she had obviously slept, she looked like the dead. Dark rings underlined her eyes, and her back and shoulders were hunched in pain.

"Good morning," I replied. "How's your foot?"

"Sore, but OK," she answered. "Some exercise should do it good—and, yes, I will be gentle on it."

I gave her a smile, knowing that nothing would stop her from journeying.

"Mirrakin's left us," I said quietly.

"No surprises there," she sighed.

"He doesn't think we'll make it across the Misran," I continued, "and he seriously doubts that Father Bruëll will help us."

"Hmm," pondered Riola, "I'm not sure if those are really his reasons for running away."

"Oh? Why's that?"

"Well, I think he's afraid that we will find Father Bruëll, that he will help us. From what I've heard, many people fear him. I think that's because they don't understand him. If he's the type of person who sees you for who you really are—that's very scary for some."

"Should we fear him?"

"No, you don't have to fear Father Bruëll. No matter how powerful he may be, I think he's also wise—very wise.

"Strange," I said after a pause, "I can't imagine Mirrakin being afraid of anything. He seems so strong and courageous. Did you see how he attacked the Myurim last night?"

"Don't forget that the trolls helped," replied Riola. "He's brave when it comes to battles, but fearful in many other ways. He is human, after all, like you and me."

I saw the wisdom in Riola's words. Mirrakin was only human, and I hadn't had his tough life. Deep inside, though, I yearned to have his courage. I felt so small compared to him.

"I know," I replied with a sigh, "you're probably right. It's just that…well, I wish I could be brave. I wish I could stand up and fight. I wish I could be awake, alert, and see danger ahead like he does."

"Wow, that's a lot of big wishes!" she exclaimed with a smile. "Cole, one day I think you'll become all you want to be, maybe even more. For now, you've got a lot to learn. Remember, this isn't the world that you come from—don't be too hard on yourself."

"I suppose you're right. I see him as almost superhuman, and I didn't realize that he might actually fear Father Bruëll. But he did say something that made sense; he said that a powerful king wouldn't bother with us. He's probably right you know - we're two nobodies. If we actually make it across that desert and find Father Bruëll, do you *really* think he'll help us? Be honest. What are my chances of making it back to Mum and Dad, or even Earth?

Riola looked me in the eyes with a sober, focused expression.

"I can't answer that, Cole, but nothing comes without a fight, nothing."

There was a certain tone in her voice that scared me; it was a lot less positive than I expected. Did she also doubt? I felt something inside my soul shift or harden, almost as if bracing for the worst. Riola was weary and badly injured. Mirrakin had abandoned us. Father Bruëll was beginning to feel like a vanishing hope. *I'm going to end up fighting this out alone*, I thought to myself. *Why didn't I see it coming? I'm so blind.* I took in a deep breath and exhaled slowly. Riola reached out and gave my shoulder a gentle squeeze.

"Come on," she said. "There's no use in hanging around here. We need some breakfast, then we should head for the Misran. If you wake up the trolls and start packing our stuff, I'll make something for us to eat."

I ambled over to the trolls and found Bella already awake. She had wandered a few feet from the others to forage between the roots of a tree. Luckily the chain had stopped her from going too far. Humphrey and Mrs. P, on the other hand, were still snoring blissfully.

"Hey, you two," I said, "it's time to get up!"

When I got no response, I decided to lift their chain and tug at it as hard as I could. They still didn't respond; the weight of the trolls was far too much to move, even with my best efforts. I flopped to the ground in frustration and stared up at the trees.

"Well, my smelly friends," I said, "this is the last spot of shade you'll enjoy for at least a few days; there's nothing in the Misran besides barren sand!"

A few minutes later, I tried again to wake the two sleepyheads. As I turned to Mrs. P, I noticed that she was wide awake, staring intently into the trees beyond the campsite. I followed the line of her gaze, but I couldn't see what had caught her attention.

"What are you looking at?" I asked quietly.

Suddenly Humphrey snorted and woke up. He raised his head, then remained absolutely still, only his nose and ears twitching slightly. After a moment or two, he heaved his great weight off the ground and peered about cautiously. By then, Bella had also realized that something was amiss; she stopped her eating and sniffed the air.

"What on earth have you discovered?" I whispered.

Looking back, I'm not sure that the two trolls woke up because they perceived something in their sleep—previously, it had taken the bellow of a Myurim to rouse them. They probably woke up naturally, then felt the presence of something malicious. Either way, I was very unsettled. They sensed something, and I couldn't see what it was. I got to my feet and scanned the area, determined to pick out anything suspicious. In a clump of trees several yards away, a slight movement caught my attention. High up in the branches, a large, coiled snake had its eyes fixed on us. I looked hard at the creature and noticed that it was emerald green, exactly the color of the snakes that had spied on me in the market.

As soon as the python realized that it had been seen, it disappeared into the foliage. A cold chill ran down my spine. "Oh, no!" I exclaimed under my breath. "How long was it watching us?"

I ran over to Riola in a panic. She had diligently packed all of our belongings and was busy laying out some of the cured meats.

"Are the trolls awake now?" she asked.

"Riola," I interrupted, "a snake has been spying on us! It was in a tree not too far from the trolls. The nasty thing slithered off as soon as I saw it."

"Are you sure it was a snake and not just a vine or something?"

"Very! The trolls acted strangely, too—they knew it was there. It was exactly the same color as the two I saw in the market. Mirrakin said they're the servants of the evil lord."

"Oh great," she replied, "this isn't going to be easy. It will call for reinforcements, and I wouldn't be surprised if it saw us kill the Myurim last night. We'd better get going now, or we may not even reach the Misran!"

"And how do we travel under the desert sun?" I asked. "Will the trolls be able to cope?"

"There's no choice," she replied. "We'll have to tie covers over their eyes to keep out the light, and we must carry as much water as possible."

"We could hide for a while," I suggested, "or even leave this evening, when all is clear."

"No, Cole, we'd be sniffed out. We have to make it to the oasis as fast as we can. I'm not getting put in prison again. Besides, Lord Urratä may not pursue us into the desert—he knows that most creatures don't survive out there. It may be the safest place for us right now."

"But what about Lord Grimmon? He's going to try stop us, right? Mirrakin said that there are worse creatures out there than the Myurim. He said our battles had only begun! We need to think about what we're up against. We need some sort of plan."

Riola dropped her head and stared at the ground.

"Well," she eventually replied, "there are creatures much worse than the Myurim, and Lord Grimmon will definitely oppose us, but there's no point in discussing that now. You can plan all you like, Cole. It probably won't help much. All I know is that we have to get across that desert, and we have to do it as fast as we can."

She marched off to finish preparing the meal. Once we had eaten, I filled the water bottles while Riola hastily loaded our luggage onto the trolls. When the time came to place eye covers on them, the creatures kicked up a real fuss. Mrs. P kept trying to rub hers off, and Humphrey took a lot of convincing and coaxing. It wasn't an easy job. The material had to be securely fastened, but we also needed to leave small gaps—so that they could see the ground just ahead of them. In the end, we won the tug-of-war, and the trolls were ready for the trek ahead.

Before we started our journey, I took out the sword and held it tight. The handle was a little too large for me, but I could do nothing about that. I swung the blade from side to side, feeling its weight as it sliced the air.

Swoosh!

Swoosh!

Real swords had never been a part of my world—I felt silly and out of place. Deep in my soul, my wavering courage battled the whispering voice of fear.

"I won't be able to use this sword in a battle. I couldn't even fight

off the Myurim; how will I face anything worse? And surely the trolls will collapse in the heat. Mirrakin was wise to go his own way. I should've followed him!"

"Come on, Cole!" yelled Riola. "We need to leave now. Put that sword away, and let's get going."

The sharp sound of her voice snapped me back into reality.

"How long will it take us to reach the desert?" I asked.

"I'm not sure," she replied. "Mirrakin thought about an hour or two."

When we left, the gorge descended steeply for a while longer, and slippery boulders dotted the path. Like the night before, I spent a lot of time trying to help the trolls, though it was much harder without Mirrakin. Humphrey and Bella became more and more uncooperative as the heat of the day increased, and Mrs. P grumbled the entire time. Riola struggled on in silence. Even with her badly hurting foot, she never asked for help.

To balance all of these woes, we had the stream. It bubbled along beside us the whole way down, and we stopped as often as we could to take a drink or to splash the trolls.

As we descended, the gorge widened out. Small thorny bushes replaced the clumps of trees, and the smooth boulders gave way to sharp rocks and stones. The stream eventually arrived at a pool wedged between two enormous rocky outcrops. We had finally reached the edge of the Misran. Before us, stretching from east to west, lay a flat wasteland of scorched sand. To the north, far, far to the north, was a sliver of land, a mere blurred line.

"What's that on the horizon?" I asked.

"That's where we're headed," replied Riola. "Those are mountains, and on the other side of them are the lands of Father Bruëll."

"Wow, that tiny smudge is a range of mountains! How far away is it?"

"I'm not sure, Cole, I just hope it's a lot closer than it looks."

"So do I, but if that *is* our destination, I never imagined we'd see it today!"

Humphrey and his friends had collapsed in a heap right beside the pool. Riola untied their bags and let them wade into the water.

"This is perfect," she said with a smile. "Their skin will need this before we trudge into that sand. We should have a quick rest, too. My foot is starting to throb."

"Will you be able to keep going?" I asked.

"Yes, of course I will," she replied. "I haven't come all this way to give up now."

After we had cooled ourselves off in the water, we had a quick bite to eat. Then Riola packed things up and called the trolls.

"Let's get a move on," she instructed. "I don't want Lord Urratä's guards to gain ground on us. If there is an oasis out there, we need to reach it before nightfall—it'll be no good looking for water in the dark."

The trolls grunted and groaned as they hauled themselves out of the pool—Humphrey and Bella had taken to being completely submerged. Once they were ready and loaded with luggage, we headed for the sand. All of a sudden, however, we heard yelling.

"*Mywan yaheed!*"

"*Mywan yaheed!*"

"Run!" screamed Riola.

But it was too late.

As quiet as could be, the sentries had climbed down the gorge behind us. When their officer yelled the final command, we were well within reach. Riola and the trolls scattered to the left, while I bolted to the right. Before I could even make for cover, a large, rough hand caught my wrist and pulled me back with a jerk. Flung to the ground, I landed face down with a thud. My captor pounced on top of me, pulled my hands behind my back, and began binding them.

In the background, I could hear the trolls bellowing, the sentries yelling commands, and Riola screaming.

"Leave them alone! Leave them alone!"

Her cries soon died away, and I assumed that she had been caught and gagged. We had lost. The journey was over. With my face pushed into the dirt, my heart sank.

"Small and annoying is the pestilence!"

Huh, I wondered, *whose voice was that?*

My captor, still busy tying me up, suddenly dropped the ropes and ran off. Some kind of skirmish had apparently erupted nearby. The sound of rocks crashing and wood breaking filled the air. I could hear the chaos of people running to and fro.

"They must leave the little ones alone. Bullies they are, each and every one, but cowards at heart, I tell you, cowards at heart!"

There it was again, the strange voice booming out over all the noise. I pulled myself onto my feet, struggled out of the ropes, and looked about.

I was startled to see a great giant lurching about, armed with the trunk of a small tree. He took determined swipes at the sentries, sending them flying in every direction. Shields crumpled, swords bent, and helmets fell to the ground like discarded rubble. Within a matter of minutes, a handful of soldiers were trying desperately to make their way back to the gorge. There was little point. The giant strode single-mindedly after them. More cries of pain rang out as he hurled them into the trees and surrounding foliage.

Directly across from where I stood, I saw Riola sitting on a rock, staring aghast at the scene. The trolls were covered in a mat of ropes, none of them securely fastened—the soldiers hadn't had the time. I stumbled across to her and sat down.

"Wh-who on earth… i-is that?" I spluttered.

"I have no idea," she replied, "but he's very welcome. He seems to be on our side!"

A minute or two later, the giant came striding over. His thin, sinewy body towered above us, and his weather-beaten skin was a light sandy color. Although he was bald, his face was unusually hairy, with thick, knotted eyebrows, large ears that sprouted great wisps of hair, and a beard at least two feet long. He wore a tattered, sack-like garment and, despite being barefoot, he seemed completely unaffected by the sharp gravel and rocks. He sat down beside us, resting the tree trunk he carried on the ground. A gentle smell of ginger perfumed the air about him.

"Lots of armor, lots of buckles, lots of bows," he announced gravely. "Each the same, nonetheless, and cowards, I tell you."

"Thank you very much," said Riola. "You saved our lives!"

"The least I could do," replied the giant, "the very least I could do. No one likes to see him win, the one who is inside out."

"The one who is inside out," I repeated. "Who's that?"

The giant appeared startled by my question and looked at me square in the eyes.

"Has my Small Lord not heard of the one by the name of Grimmon?"

"Yes, I have," I replied fervently, "but weren't those the soldiers of Lord Urratä?"

"Pah!" scorned the giant. "Lord Urratä is no more than the glove of Lord Grimmon."

Neither of us knew quite what to say. No one had told us that a giant inhabited the area, and his sheer presence was a little overwhelming.

"I see that you have made the Decision," he declared solemnly.

"Made what decision?" I queried.

"To travel to the Father. That is your reason for entering the Misran, is it not? Few other reasons there are."

"Yes, we do hope to find Father Bruëll..."

"Indeed, my Small Lord, and you are no coward."

"What is your name?" I asked, hoping that I hadn't been too bold.

"My name," came the humble reply, "is Taurn."

"Torn...Taurn, that's a lovely name. Am I saying it right?"

"Yes, that is correct, but not so loudly—at least not in these parts! Some are unaware that I am here."

"Who doesn't know you're here?"

Taurn sat quietly, staring out across the desert. A large tear rolled out of his eye, passed over his cheek, and landed with a splash on the dry earth beneath.

"Never mind," he replied glumly, "never mind."

There was something intriguing about him; his eyes told a story. I couldn't contain my curiosity.

"Who are you?" I asked hesitantly.

"Oh why?" sighed the giant. "Of all the questions possible, my Small Lord pursues the hardest. I am a king. I am well and truly a king, though neither you nor anyone else would know it."

"A king? Wow. Where's your kingdom?"

"Not too far from here, but not too close, either. Some twisting, some turning, a little journeying, and we would be there."

I believed Taurn; everything about him appeared to be honest. I continued to question him, mostly out of a desire to help.

"How did you come to be here?"

"Many vexing questions has my Small Lord, many questions," he answered. "All this land is now a blunder; doors lie open that should be closed, and bolted closed are those that should be open. There is no one here or there; we have each lost our place."

"What? You mean you've lost your place in life?"

"Indeed, my Small Lord. A tiny temptation proved a stumbling block for my feet; I passed through a door, and now I cannot retreat."

"Oh poor you; you're stuck here, aren't you?"

Taurn just nodded sadly.

"Well, if you know of Father Bruëll," I suggested, "then surely he could help you?"

"Of that I am sure. Yet, as you see, your servant is now thin and gaunt and covered in shame. I am too shy to plead to the King, for I have been hiding for so many years. Hiding is what I now do, but you are bold, my Small Lord, so follow your path."

"I hope you'll join us one day," I replied. "It would be lovely to see you again."

Once more the mysterious giant became quiet, so there the three of us sat, looking out over the horizon and resting our weary bodies.

All of a sudden, he broke the silence, springing to his feet.

"I beg your pardon, my Small Ones. I have kept you waiting. You must not tarry; you must leave now! Lord Grimmon does not take a liking to those who fight, or use their wills. He prefers the weak, those who sleep, floating a little here, floating a little there, but never somewhere."

"Do you know where Father Bruëll is?" asked Riola. "I've heard he's on the other side of those mountains. If he is, would you give us a little help, or perhaps a clue—that range is huge!"

"Yes, of course I would," replied Taurn with a glint in his eye. He knelt right down beside her, stretched out a long, thin arm, and pointed into the horizon.

"There, my Small Princess, head for the highest peak and you'll not go wrong. Be always aware and do not tarry, for you are surely followed."

"What—followed by more soldiers?" I groaned.

"Perhaps soldiers, perhaps birds, perhaps whatever," replied the giant. "It is all a chase for those who desire to leave, and I cannot defend my Small Ones forever."

He got up and tiptoed towards the two great outcroppings of rock at the foot of the pool.

"Do not tarry!" he advised one last time.

And then, to our astonishment, he squeezed his entire body into the small gap between the enormous rocks. He looked like an octopus disappearing into a cleft; his bones unlocked and displaced as needed, until not one inch of his stringy frame was to be seen.

"How in the world did he manage that?" I exclaimed.

"No idea, but we sure are lucky," sighed Riola. "We would've been in a real mess if it weren't for him."

"Yes, we would've," I replied. "First he came to our rescue, then he told us which direction to take."

We finally headed into the desert after that. Despite being shaken, we were relieved that we weren't in prison again. Lord Urratä had actually chased us all the way to the Misran—I hadn't really thought that would happen. But then again, who would have thought that a giant would come to our rescue? *Perhaps there'll be more like Taurn*, I thought to myself. *Perhaps we will make it.*

Before we set off, something strange happened, something I never mentioned to Riola. As I stepped onto the desert sand, I realized that I had left my sword behind—it had been flung from me when we were attacked by the pool. I asked Riola to wait a moment, then hastily made my way back to the spot where the soldier had pinned me down. When I arrived, I came across a shifty-looking Truark sentry.

Startled, I couldn't decide if I should run back to the others or call Taurn for help. Soon I realized that he was alone and not at all interested in fighting. He rummaged through the armor and baggage discarded by the fleeing soldiers. I stood watching for a while, wondering if he was actually a vagabond. When he finally looked up and saw me, he wasn't the slightest bit surprised or even aggressive, he simply started laughing. That was weird, but not as weird as the strange, almost vacant look in his eyes, as if there was no one there at all.

"Isn't this sweet," he roared, "blindly following a girl through a wasteland, hoping to find an imaginary father. Even if he did exist, why would he help you? It's laughable! Your friend's a little muddled and tired to the bone. I'll bet she annoys you, too, doesn't she? With that injured foot of hers…limp…limp…limp. Why are you even following her? It doesn't make sense. Ah…someone's abandoned you, haven't they? You're stuck with her."

I was too shocked to respond. *How does he know so much? How long has he been watching us?* Whether or not he attacked almost wasn't relevant; the real issue was the strange darkness that surrounded him.

"Be on your guard!" I said quietly to myself. "Be on your guard!"

I glanced about and spotted the sword a few feet away. I knew very well that it would be silly to make a dash for it.

"If I were you," continued the sentry, "I'd give the journey a miss altogether. Go your own way and save yourself. You've no idea how many people I've seen die trying to cross that desert. If you're foolishly hoping for an oasis, forget it. It's a nasty suspicion, but I have a feeling that I'll be rummaging through your baggage tomorrow."

With that, he burst out laughing again and began picking his way between the bushes back towards the gorge.

When he was some way off, I grabbed the sword and ran back to the others as fast as my legs would carry me. Riola noticed that I was a little pale, but I told her I was just tired. It would have been pointless to say anything more; she had decided to go ahead with the journey, and that was that.

Thinking about the event a little later, I realized that the sentry hadn't said a word in Truark—he had known what language I spoke. A cold shiver ran down my spine. Was he a dark messenger, sent to fill me with fear? If that was true, it had worked. Even though I knew his words were twisted, I couldn't help wondering if Riola had got things confused. Were we going to meet our ruin? Would she actually betray me? The more I questioned our fate, the more Taurn's encouragements faded.

"It's just like I thought," I whispered to myself. "I'll end up fighting it out alone."

CHAPTER ELEVEN:

A Wasteland
══o○o══

Although the sun was slowly descending, its rays were relentless. A bright glare reflected off the sand. Even with their eye covers on, the trolls could barely cope. To make things worse, the sand was hot, soft and deep. Our feet sank with every step that we took, and our muscles ached from the effort of it all. It drained our strength, leaving our legs feeling heavier than lead. The whole experience was probably even worse for the trolls. Their great chain weighed them down as it ploughed along, leaving obvious tracks for anyone who wanted to follow us. *Huff, puff, huff, puff,* the poor creatures went. We only managed to keep going, step by step, through sheer determination and the constant fear of being caught.

Riola stopped after an hour or so, took out some of the blankets, and threw them over the backs of the trolls.

"I should've done that earlier," she said wearily. "We don't need them getting sunstroke!"

She also gave them some water, and we drank from our own bottles. I felt like gulping down the whole lot, but she warned me to drink sparingly—we would have to make it last. Then our slow march continued, deeper and deeper into the wasteland.

Riola was limping badly by then. The bandage around her foot refused to stay on, so a lot of grit and sand had worked its way into the wound. She was exhausted, and in a lot of pain. The words of the deranged sentry played over and over in my mind: "*You've no idea how many people I've seen die trying to cross that desert...*" I could almost hear his coarse laughter and see the look of mockery in his eyes. Fear crept into my imagination, and I became more and more certain that we would never make it alive.

I paused and turned around to view our trail; it wound its way through the sand as far as the eye could see. The gorge where we'd started had long since disappeared.

"Well, if someone wants to come after us," I said aloud, "they won't find it difficult; our tracks are unmistakable."

"We'll have to keep going regardless," mumbled Riola. "The further we travel, the better."

"Why don't you ride on Humphrey?" I suggested. "Your foot looks really bad."

"If I do ride on him," she replied abruptly, "I'll exhaust him. The trolls find this sand much harder to cope with than we do."

She put her head down and pushed on.

Before long we really started to work on each other's nerves. Anger clouded my mind.

"Stupid," I muttered with annoyance, "so darn stupid! It's her way or the highway. That sentry was right. She's deluded; this Father Bruëll stuff is a load of rubbish. I'm dropping her as soon as I can. I'm finding my own way home."

I tried to snap out of my dark mood by recalling Taurn's encouragements. It didn't help. Negative thoughts came all too easily in that dry, horrible place. And when we stopped to rest, or to drink some water, we didn't say a word to each other.

I held onto one small spark of encouragement.

The mountain range to the north had increased in size, as the sun's harshness decreased with every passing minute. This relieved our burnt skin, but the dwindling light soon became a real worry. With no path to follow, we relied on the distant haze of the mountains to keep us travelling in the right direction. Finding our way in the dark would be impossible. Neither of us knew how to get our bearings from the stars.

I stopped to scan the horizon and saw something ahead of us.

"What do you think that is?" I called to Riola.

She looked up from her monotonous march and peered into the distance. There clearly was something there—a small blotch that could've been a clump of trees.

"Well," she answered, "that may be the oasis."

"Hmm," I pondered aloud, "either that, or it's another nasty surprise."

"Whatever it is," she replied, "let it wait; we're not turning back now."

I lifted my eyes to the sky and there, high above, I saw a number of little dots.

"Oh no!" I exclaimed. "Look up! I bet those are giant crows."

"Darn it, you could be right!" she said angrily. "Well, we were expecting something. Even Taurn warned us."

"So now what?" I asked fearfully. "We can't run; we'll have to fight!"

"Cole, I don't have the energy to fight. There are at least five of them, and the trolls will be useless in this sand."

"We have to fight, Riola! It's either that, or we let ourselves get pecked to death!"

Before she could answer, a light wind picked up. Gentle at first, it gathered strength, sweeping grains of sand along in its path. Within a few minutes, it was a pelting gale.

"The perfect cover," I spluttered over the noise of the storm. "There's no way they can fly through this."

"Probably not," she shouted. "That means we need to get to the oasis before it's over—and I do hope it's an oasis!"

In the end, the giant birds must have decided to abandon their attack. We pressed on, keeping our heads low to avoid the wind and sand. In spite of our efforts, little pieces of grit made their way into our eyes, ears, pockets, and bags. Coughing, spluttering, groaning, and sneezing, we journeyed on. After an hour or so, the wind finally died down, and we were able to lift our heads. To our astonishment, a large grove lay a few yards ahead.

Most of the trees were either dead or dying, but we stopped in our tracks and took in the sight. An enormous flock of bright little blue birds, each with an orange bill, swooped from tree to tree. They rose into the air in unison, fluttered about, and then dropped down to settle in a tree before taking off again. What a beautiful display of color they were!

"It doesn't look like much," I said, "but I guess that's the oasis."

"Yes," agreed Riola, "that must be it."

"And the storm will have blown away our tracks," I continued. "That should make things a lot harder for anyone who wants to find us. What do you think?"

"I'm not so sure. This is the one place where travelers can rest around here, and the crows were onto us a little while ago. They know we'll be here."

Well, I thought with a smile, *She's probably right, but at least the filthy sentry was a liar—there is an oasis after all!*

The trolls, realizing that an opportunity to relax had arrived, collapsed in a heap and fell asleep. Riola and I couldn't decide whether or not we should enter the grove.

"Do you think it's safe?" I asked.

"Not sure," she answered. "Anything could be hiding in there."

Eventually, I decided to end the deliberation. I pulled out the sword. "I'll creep in quietly and have a look. It'll be easier if I go alone. You stay here with the trolls."

"OK. I'm too tired to go a step further anyway, and my foot is in agony. I'll keep watch from here."

With the sword raised, I carefully approached the grove, entering as quietly as possible. Dry twigs and sticks littered the ground, and I had to be very careful not to step on any of them. I didn't want a loud cracking sound to announce my presence. Through the dry foliage I soon caught sight of a single healthy tree, large, sturdy, and covered in leaves. If there was anyone about, they'd most likely be there. I tightened my grip on the sword and prepared for the worst.

Out of the corner of my eye, I spotted a large lizard scurrying down the trunk of a dead tree. It paused for a moment, probed the air with its tongue, and darted off. For me, there was no escape, no running away; my next confrontation lay ahead. Crouching as low as I could, I edged forward. *Crunch, crunch, crunch* went my feet on the dry earth and gravel.

"Oh be quiet!" I whispered to myself. "Don't go and mess it up now."

When I got within a few yards of the flourishing tree, I hid behind a shrub and peered at the scene. An old man sat at the base of the trunk. I stared long and hard at him, trying to figure out whether or not he was peaceful. I could see that he was more than old; he was ancient. And the beautiful green tree, massive and sturdy as it was, looked equally old. Large, twisted roots poured out from its base, winding their way here and there before plunging into the earth. Many smaller trunks, all woven and knotted together as they reached up into the sky, made up an enormous main trunk. The chaotic branches sprawled in every direction, as if each was desperate to find its own growing space. The thick, dense, deep green leaves hardly belonged in a dying oasis.

I had no idea what to do next. *Where's my courage?*

Having a sword was all very well, but was the old man really alone? For all I knew, the whole thing could've been a trap. In the end, the decision was made for me.

"Where are the others?"

Was that his voice? I wondered. *Does he actually know I'm here?*

To be on the safe side, I didn't say a word in response—after all, the old man hadn't looked in my direction when he spoke.

"Son, where are the others? Where are your friends?" He turned and looked directly at me.

Oh…right, I thought, *that was definitely addressed to me.*

"Bring your sword if you like," he continued. "There's no need to leave it in the bushes."

"Ah…yes. Right…of course…sir," I stammered.

"You needn't call me sir," he replied with a smile. "My name is Mershnin."

I lowered my sword and sheepishly walked over to him.

His skin looked more like a hide than anything else, wrinkled, worn, and weather-beaten. A deep olive color, it covered his wiry frame and strong hands with such generosity that it ended up a size too large. Loose sacks had gathered beneath his deeply set eyes, and his nose was large and angular. He wore a simple garment and no shoes. Despite his lack of obvious wealth, he exuded a sense of peace, strength, and nobility. I noticed that his feet rested in a pool of water. It must have seeped out of the ground, or perhaps from the roots of the tree.

"The trolls would love this water," he said quietly.

"Uh, perhaps I should go and get them."

"Perhaps you should."

He whistled a gentle note, and a strikingly marked bird fluttered down from its roost to alight on his hand. Clearly, this was no ordinary man.

At that point, it occurred to me to wonder how he knew about the trolls. Did he see us arrive? Did someone betray us? Yet, somehow, that didn't fit the picture. Something about Mershnin was too solid and too strong for silly games.

Wait a minute...Mershnin. Mershnin? What was it about that name? Was this the Mershnin who defeated Khülm? Was this the Morodian general that Riola had told me about?

Chapter Twelve

Walking with a Legend

=o○o=

When I got back, I discovered that Riola had fallen asleep with the trolls. The gentle sound of snores, snorts, and quiet mutters filled the air around them. After I finally managed to wake her, I told Riola about the old man under the tree. I anticipated having a bit of trouble convincing her, but she was actually too tired to care. So, with the trolls in tow, we made our way through the dying grove. The last few rays of the sun were fast disappearing, which made navigation a little trickier than I expected.

When we arrived at the clearing beneath the great, sprawling tree, we found that Mershnin had made a fire. He introduced himself to Riola and each of the trolls, greeting them by name. That was a little surprising.

"How do you know about us?" she asked.

"Well," answered the old man, "you understand that Lord Grimmon has his ways of knowing things, right? Have you ever considered the possibility that Father Bruëll does, too?"

"No," replied Riola, "I hadn't."

"Father Bruëll knows very well who you are," continued Mershnin, "and he knows much about you, too, Cole."

"He does?" I exclaimed in surprise. "Father Bruëll knows about me?"

Before I could ask him any questions, he walked off and returned with two large urns, each filled with water. Then, while we washed our faces, hands, and feet, Mershnin saw to the trolls. He carefully unfastened their baggage, scrubbed them down, and rubbed oil on their parched hides. When he finished that, he applied ointment to Riola's wounded foot and gave her new bandages.

"You must rest now, young lady," he said in a firm, fatherly voice, "or you're going to make things a lot harder for yourself."

Once the trolls were settled and we had finished cleaning up, Mershnin prepared dinner. He told Riola to relax by the fire, and sent me on a mission to find a special type of plant. Armed with a lantern, I headed off and began searching a few yards from the campsite.

Before long, I discovered the sign that I'd been told to look for—a tiny white flower growing near the base of a dry tree. Beneath that delicate plant, I hoped to find an enormous, sweet tuber. I knelt down and scratched away at the earth. Then I felt a gentle brushing against my back.

The subtle intrusion came out of nowhere and was so slight at first that I hardly noticed anything. The second time it caught my attention, I froze. There was no point in reaching for my sword; I had left it at the campsite. Of course, I wondered if it was all in my imagination. The brushing came a third time, unmistakably. There was definitely something behind me. In a burst of courage, I jumped up and swung around, ready to face the intruder or run for my life.

A mere foot or so from where I stood was an enchanting cat. It looked like any domestic feline, only a *lot* bigger. Apart from its size, I'll never forget its striking colors. Alternating stripes of olive and earthy red covered it from head to tail, and its hair was thick and glossy. Its body was muscular, and its paws were enormous. The animal sat bolt upright, with its deep green eyes steadily focused on me.

Should I give it some attention? I wondered, *Perhaps a pat on the head?*

Something about the sheer size of this character made me uncomfortable. After a long day's walk, the last thing I wanted was a confrontation. In the end, I decided to greet the animal respectfully, then head for the campsite. That's when things got more interesting.

As soon as I tried to leave, I felt a determined tug on my left ankle. I looked down and saw that the wily creature had clawed my sock. The harder I pulled, the harder the cat pulled. This little tug of war carried on for a minute or so before I realized that I'd been taken prisoner. Naturally, I bent down to try to coax the animal to release its hold—no amount of pleading worked. Next, I put my lantern down and carefully tried to untangle the cat's claws from the fibers of my sock. Strangely enough, it let me do this. I soon learned that it was all part of a cunning plan. The moment I put all of my effort into freeing my sock, the feline released its hold and jumped right up onto my shoulders. There it sat, holding on with the full grip of every claw and purring loudly.

"Ouch!"

Purr.

"Ouch!"

I had been outwitted.

I returned to the camp, tuber in one hand, lantern in the other, and the enormous cat stretched across my shoulders.

"Wow," said Mershnin with a laugh, "you've collected more than I asked for!"

"Yes," I replied sheepishly, "I've made a friend."

"At least it's not a python this time!" chuckled Riola.

"Very funny. What do you call this animal?" I asked.

"That's a Horbinn Cat," answered Mershnin with delight.

"So, it's just a cat?" I queried.

"I wouldn't say it's *just* a cat," he replied. "They're the most wily of all animals in these parts—somewhat unpredictable, yet good-natured. A few pass across the Misran at night. During the day, they either bury themselves in the sand, or they spend time in this oasis."

"So typical," I said with a sigh, "problematic animals must have a thing for me."

"Not at all," responded Mershnin. "This is a blessing. They say that you only see a Horbinn Cat if it means to be seen. That one obviously trusts you, which is a good sign."

"A good sign? Really? It practically trapped me, and now I can't get it off."

"Cole, you must ask him to get off."

"Ask him to? I pleaded with him to let go of me when he first latched onto my sock. He completely ignored me!"

In the meantime, the curious creature had made itself quite comfortable on my shoulders. In fact, it looked to be settling in for the night. Out of pure curiosity, the trolls wandered over and stood watching from a few feet away.

Under Mershnin's guidance, I spoke to the cat in a polite, firm voice, asking him to jump down. Nothing happened. Eventually, my voice must have hit the right tone, because all of a sudden, the animal jumped to the ground without any protest and headed straight for the warmth of the fire. There it curled up into a tight ball and went to sleep.

"Ow! I'm sore," I exclaimed. "He's got sharp claws."

"Remember," said Mershnin, "he's no ordinary cat. Anyway, now that you're free, you can help me prepare dinner."

We diced the tuber that I had dug up and threw the pieces into a large clay pot resting near the center of the fire. A wonderful, rich aroma drifted into the air when he lifted the lid. Riola and I suddenly felt starving. We had forgotten what a good meal looked like. That night, we each ate enough for three people, finishing the entire stew in less than a few minutes, and leaving the pot thoroughly scraped of every last morsel.

When we'd eaten dinner and cleaned the pot, we gathered our blankets and huddled around the fire. The air was absolutely still. I can't remember falling asleep that night, and I can't remember a thing I dreamt, either, but I woke up late the next morning. Mershnin, on the other hand, must have faithfully woken up several times to place fresh logs on the fire; the Misran was as cold at night as it was hot during the day. While we ate breakfast, Mershnin told us that we wouldn't be leaving the grove that day. Riola tried to disagree, but the old sage warned her that she hadn't rested enough. He told me that I needed some training, and we wouldn't be going anywhere until I had received it.

Before we got going with the day's activities, Mershnin explained how the desert had once been a magnificent forest, filled with more species of birds, animals, and insects than could be counted.

One landmark remained to bear witness to this, and that was the dying grove with its single, sturdy tree. The old sage also told us about his years as a general in the proud Morodian army. He recounted how he and Truwen had escaped the anger of the Morodian government by travelling far north until they reached the lands of Father Bruëll.

Riola and I hung on every word—the old man had lived an extraordinary life. However, the more he spoke, the more I wanted to ask questions. Why was he marooned in a wasteland? What had happened to Truwen? How does a thriving forest get turned into a desert? Kind and patient, Mershnin answered each question as well as he could.

When they entered his kingdom, Father Bruëll welcomed the forlorn soldier and his wife. They were, to say the least, destitute. Mershnin had been stripped of his rank and title, declared an outlaw, and forbidden to return to Morodia. With nothing to lose, they had even considered seeking refuge with Truwen's father, but Truwen herself had finally decided against this. She had told Mershnin the truth about how her father had sent her to ask for a job as a chambermaid, and how he had carefully instructed her to lead the general away from his military duties. When she agreed to the plan, it never crossed her mind that she might fall in love with the general. Obviously, it would've been foolish to mention this to Drimmik— he might well have tried to use her love in another plot against his enemies. All in all, it was better to keep a safe distance from both Morodia and the Truarks.

Father Bruëll understood the young couple's plight. Yes, they had been impulsive, and perhaps irresponsible, but their own cultures were far from honest or wise. Father Bruëll could see both sides of the story, and he offered Mershnin and Truwen compassion. He knew that they had become aliens in a foreign land, with nowhere to call home. Furthermore, Father Bruëll understood the greater story, the story of the collapse of that world, and of the determined, cunning arrival of Lord Grimmon.

That morning, Mershnin told us why the war against Khülm had been a mistake, and how it had left the country without honest leadership. He described how Lord Grimmon had been waiting patiently for many years to find a way into Khülm. When the fighting started, he had been delighted. He had been even more delighted when the Khülm leadership asked the Truarks for help. They were a weak tribe, easily seduced, and Lord Grimmon knew this all too well. As far as the Truarks could tell, on one particular day, a well-dressed, well-spoken man arrived. With polite words and perfect manners, he offered their leadership support and money in return for land, and they gladly took the opportunity. As each of the weak-willed Truark warlords fell to his deceptions, Lord Grimmon spread his dark power throughout the region, starting with the Misran valley.

Under his orders, tranquil landscapes were ruthlessly mined for every last mineral, and welcoming villages were uprooted, or simply abandoned. Huge structures of iron replaced quaint houses, rusted machinery littered the fields, and dirty pools of waste collected in the shadows. Many species of birds, once common in the Misran, soon faded into extinction. Trees no longer pollinated, and their roots began to rot and die. One by one, ancient and glorious specimens withered and fell. And all that time, the mindless warlords squabbled and fought amongst themselves over who had the most power. Sadly, of course, having fallen under Lord Grimmon's spell, none were able to see clearly. During that period, people barely noticed that dry winds had been carrying in more and more sand. Within a few years, a desert had swallowed up the valley.

"Where are all those warlords now?" I asked, struggling to get my head around the way the land had been destroyed.

"They've been moving further and further south," replied Mershnin, "and they take Lord Grimmon's chaos and darkness wherever they go. Mirrakin will have told you about Lord Urratä, who rules the Khülm Trading Ruins; there are many more like him if you care to look."

"So you know Mirrakin!" exclaimed Riola. "Do you also know about how we were captured in the market?"

"Yes," replied the old sage, "as does Father Bruëll. He knows about your time in the cellar and, Riola, he even knows about how you were sold as a slave to the mines. He's been keeping an eye on you. You may struggle to see it, but there were many times when he helped you on your journey. Anyway, that's enough said for now. You'll learn more when the two of you meet him."

"What?" I asked in surprise. "He wants to meet us?"

"Why wouldn't he? He knows all too well what you've been through, and yes, he knows about your parents. As I said, Lord Grimmon isn't the only one with a watchful eye. When Truwen and I first met Father Bruëll, we had no idea what to expect - pure desperation drove us to take a chance and seek his help. As it turned out, he anticipated our arrival and took us in without question."

"So, he'll help me find my mum and dad?"

"Yes, Cole, he'll most certainly help you find your parents. I can't say how or when; those are questions he will answer. However, I can tell you what he did for us."

I felt a wave of hope and relief pass over me as Mershnin described how he and Truwen rebuilt their lives under Father Bruëll's protection. They learned about the affairs of the kingdom, and they faithfully served in the Royal Courts. There, they tended to all kinds of matters, restoring their dignity. They also raised a family, and their children grew up strong and free in the palace grounds. Once these sons and daughters had left home, Father Bruëll gave the couple one final task.

When the darkness of Lord Grimmon descended on Khülm, Father Bruëll sent Mershnin and his wife to the Misran desert, to live in the grove. They would help those who wanted to escape from the oppressive rule of the dark lord. They were prefect for the job, because they knew firsthand what it was like to seek refuge in a foreign land. Year after year, they risked their lives to save those who were desperate for freedom.

To our surprise, Mershnin suddenly ended the conversation.

"My apologies—I have forgotten myself!" he exclaimed. "We have work to do."

Riola and I were a little disappointed, but the old sage moved on with determination. "Young man, you have a sword with you, do you not?" he asked.

"Yes," I replied.

"Well, then," he continued with a knowing smile, "we had better teach you how to use it!"

I found myself being coached by the most revered soldier of his time. We trained for the rest of the morning and the whole afternoon. At midday, we stopped for lunch and to take a little rest. But, by the end of the day, I had been taught how to hold the sword correctly, how to size up an enemy, how to attack, and how to defend.

More importantly, Mershin also taught me a lot about when to fight and when not to. He wisely pointed out that a sword is usually not the right answer to a conflict. Yet, when the time did come to use it, it should be handled with skill. To my surprise, he even took out his own sword, and we did some sparring. I could hardly believe that this respected sage would spend so much time and energy on me.

Riola, forbidden to do any work, spent the day sleeping beneath the tree, talking to the trolls, and studying the birds. Now and again, she also came to watch us—it was probably very amusing. With no experience, I tripped here, fell there, and spent a lot of time trying to catch my breath. And while I may have come close to giving up, I did learn to be patient with myself and to persevere.

The Horbinn Cat also watched us with fixed curiosity. His head turned this way and that with every move we made.

"That's a really strange animal," I said. "His eyes have been glued to us for most of the day."

"So he is," answered Mershnin. "Nonetheless, I have a feeling that this particular Horbinn Cat may end up helping you in battle."

"Help me in battle? Do you really mean that?"

"Absolutely, and I would gladly face an opponent with him by my side. Horbinn Cats are utterly fearless. Treat him firmly, but with respect."

At the end of the day, Mershnin reached into one of his bags and pulled out a sword. It had an amazing scabbard, wonderfully engraved.

"A gift for a warrior," he said, handing it to me. "You will need this, so keep it on your belt at all times."

I drew the weapon from its sheath and held it firmly. The shining blade balanced perfectly, and my hand molded around the hilt.

"Oh, wow," I exclaimed in disbelief, "it's magnificent!"

"You deserve it," said Mershnin. "You *truly* deserve it! Listen carefully; it is your turn to take the lead. Riola is no longer able to guide you. She is in too much pain, and Lord Grimmon has wounded her soul too deeply. Cole, you are going to have to get her to Father Bruëll. That is your task, your invitation to carve out a place in the story. Although it may seem challenging, there are things to be done before returning to Earth and your parents. You can choose to go your own way, or you can accept that you have an important role to play. Will you choose to stand up and fight? Will you be courageous?"

"Yes, sir."

I hadn't meant to say *sir*, but Mershnin's voice was so serious that it popped out of my mouth before I could stop it.

"You have not been abandoned," he continued. "It is time to reject that lie. Put it behind you. There are more allies around you now than you realize, and you're going to need them. You have joined a battle that is far larger than you could ever understand. Now, remember this; if you are ever at your wit's end, do not accept defeat—call on Father Bruëll."

"Ah…call on him?"

"Yes, simply call on him. You will understand what I mean when the time comes."

That night, we once again ate a generous dinner. The kind old sage had also prepared some supplies for the journey ahead: smoked meats, dried tubers, fruit, and extra water bottles. We sat in comfort beneath the magnificent tree, with the fire crackling in the background and the stars shining high above.

"Why can't we stay here?" asked Riola. "I'm tired of travelling."

"Stay here?" enquired Mershnin. "You wouldn't stay here if you knew what awaited you."

"Oh really? But this is so cosy and safe, just like home."

"No, Riola, you must reach your destination. Besides, I may not be here for much longer. I am an old man now—my time is nearly up."

"Will we meet Truwen?" I asked tentatively.

"Ah, my lovely wife," he replied with a smile. "No, you will not meet her, for she has already passed on. I hope to follow her soon."

"If you leave, what will become of the grove? Will it survive?"

"My dear young man, this oasis cannot last forever. Everything has its season."

Crunch.

Snap.

The distinct sound of cracking twigs caught our attention.

"That was no more than a few feet away," I whispered. Very quietly, I clutched the hilt of my sword and drew it from the scabbard.

"There's no need for that," cautioned Mershnin. "In fact, you may discover that you know our intruder very well."

A huge black panther entered the clearing, followed by an exhausted Mirrakin. Now, I had seen panthers in the zoo before, but I had never come across one in the wild. The creature was sleek, muscular, and more fearsome than anything I could have imagined. It seemed to prowl rather than walk, with its body lowered, its ears folded back, and its eyes alert and suspicious. The majestic animal glanced at me and, with a deep, rumbling growl, exposed a pair of white canines.

"Sit, Talilah, sit," commanded Mirrakin.

The panther drew off to one side and lay down, its tail swishing from side to side.

"Whoa," I gasped, "that's one mean pet!"

Mershnin offered the Truark boy and his panther some food and water. Like us, they must have been starving—they consumed the entire meal in a matter of minutes.

"So you finally decided to come," said Riola after a

moment's silence.

"I suppose I did," replied Mirrakin. "I left you in the gorge because I was, I was…"

"Fearful?" suggested Riola.

"Could be," answered Mirrakin. "I hadn't really thought of it like that."

It was a strange meeting, all in all. Few questions were asked—perhaps there wasn't a need for many words. Riola hardly seemed surprised by Mirrakin's arrival. Come to think of it, she didn't seem overjoyed, either. As I got to know her, I came to expect that; she kept her emotions to herself.

And no one asked where the panther had come from. We all knew that Mirrakin was a resourceful young man, and left it at that.

A little later in the evening, before we settled down to sleep, Mershnin pulled out a piece of paper with the words of a song.

"Truwen wrote these lyrics before she died," he said in a quiet voice, "but it has never been sung. Riola, perhaps you can have a go? I will play the flute—my voice is no good for singing."

"I would love to," she replied, "just don't expect me to sing as well as Truwen."

She looked over the words while Mershnin found the right key. When they finally began, the beauty of the melody stunned me. The day had been too long, though.

Despite fighting sleep tooth and nail, I drifted off before they even finished.

CHAPTER THIRTEEN:

The Magnificent Riders
══o◯o══

The following morning, I woke up to the sound of strange whispering. The air felt different, as if the warmth and safety of the grove had disappeared. My heart sank. Something was definitely wrong. I'd learned enough to listen for clues before moving. So, I strained my ears and focused all of my attention on the hushed voice. The mumbled sounds began to gain clarity, and I finally recognized the words.

"Abandoned, worthless, abandoned, worthless, abandoned..."

Again and again the sinister chant repeated. Very slowly, I reached for my sword and gripped the hilt—I had been sure to leave it at my side the night before. Raising my head a little, I looked around. Everyone seemed to be asleep, including Mirrakin and the panther. I sat up quietly, and saw Riola on the opposite side of the fireplace. She, too, slept, but the dark whispers were coming from a large crow looming over her.

"You again," I said under my breath. "You're not getting away with it this time."

The crow had its back to me, so I had the element of surprise. Very slowly and carefully, I stood up, sword in hand, and crept across to the horrid creature. Focused entirely on its ritual, it only heard me when I was a few feet away, raising my sword to strike. It swung around and saw me, but, as I had expected, it didn't make a sound.

The enormous bird stretched out its wings, lowered its head, and hissed. To my own surprise, I lunged at it with my blade.

"Your time's up," I yelled.

The crow darted back and took off into the air. It rose up several feet, circled me, then swooped down like a hawk going for the kill. I crouched as low as I could, waited, and then thrust my sword upward as the bird skimmed over my head. It let out a loud screech, tumbled off course, and came to rest several feet away, enraged and clearly injured. Sure that I had the upper hand, I ran straight for the crow before it could retaliate. As I did, four more of the horrid creatures dropped out of the sky. I had forgotten that there might be others. I could take on one with my sword, but I couldn't handle four.

"Help!" I yelled. "Help!"

Thankfully, the panther came bounding across the camp. It leapt into the air with a gigantic pounce, all but landing on one of the birds. The bewildered crow let out a screech and took off, narrowly avoiding the cat's enormous claws. I used the distraction as well as I could, striking out at one of the birds that had approached from my left. With a determined thrust, I managed to connect with its side. At that point, some instinct warned me of danger from behind. I swung around. Sure enough, another crow was preparing to pounce on my back.

"Mirrakin," I yelled, "we need help."

Rather than the Truark boy, the Horbinn Cat answered my call, flying through the air like a guided missile. I glimpsed a blinding storm of teeth, snarls, and fury as the cat set about dispatching two of the crows simultaneously. The sight engrossed me for a second too long, and I felt the sharp pain of a beak piercing my thigh. As I swung around to strike with my sword, a voice distracted me.

"That one is mine."

Mirrakin had finally joined the battle. The crow, caught between the two of us, darted its eyes about nervously, hissed, and then took to flight.

"Don't let it get away," he shouted. "It'll call for help."

I jumped up with all my strength and nicked the bird with the tip of my blade. It squawked in pain, still trying to flutter upward. The panther leapt into the sky, attempting to bring the bird down midflight, but our efforts came too late; the crow was well out of harm's way. Higher and higher it soared, until finally it let out a defiant screech and headed back across the desert.

"Darn," sighed Mirrakin, "we missed it…"

"At least we beat the others," I said with excitement.

"I suppose so. Cole, you need to get going. When Lord Urratä hears that the crows have failed, he'll send something larger, and Lord Grimmon will find out about this, too, so be prepared. Remember this, though; we're in the middle of the Misran, and whatever wants you has to cross the sand by air or on foot. You still have time to get ahead."

"Does that mean you're not going to join us?"

"No, not yet. I'm going to stay here for a while. I need to rest a little."

I was disappointed that Mirrakin still wished to be on his own, even though something inside me half expected it. I turned around to look for Riola, and saw her sitting beside Mershnin. Was it possible that the old sage had slept through the entire battle?

"Is he awake?" I asked, walking over to her.

"No, and I don't think he's asleep either," she replied. "I think he passed away last night."

"What? He passed away?"

"I'm afraid so. His body has no life in it, and look at the tree— the strangest thing has happened!"

Sure enough, the rugged old tree had exploded into a beautiful display of pure white blossoms. I knelt down beside Mershnin's body. His face had an expression of complete peace.

"He died so soon," I exclaimed, "and with no warning!"

"He said he couldn't stay in this wilderness forever," she replied with tears in her eyes, "and he wanted to be with Truwen as soon as possible. He must have known that his work here was done."

"I wonder if that's why the crows arrived this morning. There's no way they would've come if he was still with us."

"You've got a point, Cole. I wouldn't be surprised if this grove fades into the sand now. The seeds from those blossoms will hopefully be carried far away, and new life will begin elsewhere."

"Do we bury him before we go?"

"No, I don't think so. We will leave him as he is, with his sword at his side, beneath the tree. That's probably the way he would've wanted it."

As she said that, a light breeze blew through the grove. It arrived gently, causing the blossoms to swirl through the air like falling snow. Gradually it gained momentum, until it became a strong wind. I turned around to call Mirrakin, and saw that he was standing a few feet from us.

"Has Mershnin passed away?" he asked quietly.

"Yes," I answered, "and we must leave now, before it's too late."

"You get going," he mumbled. "I'll head out tomorrow."

"That wouldn't be wise," I replied. "You could be attacked by something."

"Let him be," said Riola. "The mountains aren't far away now; he'll come as he chooses."

She got up to pack our belongings. Before I went to help her, I gave Mirrakin the advice that Mershnin had given me; that he should call on Father Bruëll if he was ever at his wits' end.

The wind blew harder and harder, lifting the desert sand into the sky. Riola and I worked quickly to prepare the trolls for the journey. As soon as we were ready, we called a final farewell to Mirrakin. He made his way over to us with the panther by his side.

"Don't worry," he said with a smile, "I have Talilah with me; we'll be fine. Have a safe journey, and I'll see you soon."

Riola, the trolls, and I made our way out of the grove and into the Misran. We hadn't travelled more than a few yards, when the Horbinn Cat came bounding out of the trees. It jumped right onto Bella's back and settled down for the ride.

"Glad to have you," I whispered. "You're one tough cat!"

I paid close attention to the sky and horizon—another attack was sure to come soon.

"I hope this wind is strong enough to cover our tracks," I said to Riola. "We're going to need all the help we can get."

"It may, but it may not," she replied. "Either way, we need to hurry—Lord Urratä knows where we're headed."

As we pushed on, the wind died down. After about half an hour, the air was dead still and absolutely silent. The horizon shimmered under the sun's merciless rays. Before long, my mouth felt as dry as sandpaper, and my eyes burned from the intense glare that reflected off the sand. We draped our blankets over our heads, trying desperately to shield our faces and necks from the searing heat. Every step was an effort, and the trolls winced at the pain and dryness of it all.

"Strange," said Riola, "my feet feel like they're sinking deeper and deeper."

"I think you're right," I replied. "The sand must be getting softer. How are the trolls going to manage if it carries on like this?"

"They won't," she sighed, "and neither will I—my legs feel like lead. I'm not sure which is worse; this deathly heat and fine sand, or the windstorm we faced on our way to the oasis."

"At least the windstorm covered our tracks," I replied, "and it hid us, too. Anything in the air, or on the ground, can see us now. We might as well paint targets on ourselves, and—"

"Oh look," interjected Riola, "look over there."

I raised my head and saw a dark blotch lying across our path, perhaps forty feet away.

"What is it?" I asked, coming to a stop.

"Not sure," she answered. "It's almost deep blue, and it appears to be glistening—so strange. Do you think it could be water?"

"Out here? Not very likely, not likely at all."

"Why not? What else is it, a rock? It's definitely not an animal; it's way too flat. But if it is a rock, maybe there's a spring beneath; you never know."

"Riola, if that's the case, where are the plants? It would be an oasis. Anyway, we could stand here for ages and try to guess. Let's just be careful, whatever it is."

We continued cautiously, our feet sinking deeper as we went.

"I think it's definitely water," said Riola as we got closer, "and what a gift! The trolls could use some moisture right now, and I have to stop or I'll really injure myself."

"Hang on," I replied as I pulled out my sword. "Let me have a look first."

Very slowly, I approached the dark shape. When I reached the edge of it, I leaned over and saw a reflection of my face. Even though the surface did appear to be wet, it certainly wasn't a pool. It could have been a large, flat rock with a spring beneath—perhaps Riola was right after all. If that were true, a little digging would get us lots of fresh water. Nevertheless, I was suspicious enough not to trust anything. So, with the greatest caution, I lowered the tip of my sword and gave it a gentle prodding.

Sshhh.

Squeeze.

"Aargh!" I cried out. "Something's wrapped itself around my foot!"

The Horbinn Cat let out a great hiss and stalked over with its hair on end. In the meantime, my foot was pulled deeper into the sand and a surge of pain shot up through my leg.

"What's going on?" I screamed in fright. "I can't get away!"

"Stab!" cried Riola. "Stab the sand! It's a trap!"

I plunged my sword again and again into the area around my feet. Sure enough, it connected with something. All of a sudden, the deep blue reflection changed to red and then to black. A deafening squeal pierced the air. Then a whoosh; an enormous wave of sand flew up into our faces. Through watering eyes, we saw a huge pair of batlike wings unfold into the sky, followed by a grimacing head and a long, scaly body. The creature reared up on its talons and hissed in rage. What a ghastly sight it was! Its body reminded me of a deep sea fish; glass-like and spiny, with large black eyes in bony sockets, an oversized angular head, and a wide grimacing mouth, mostly all teeth. A long tail flicked out from behind it, swishing from side to side like an angry cat. Halfway down this tail were two serrated spines.

Pulling myself out of my frozen state of shock, I frantically tried to wipe the remaining sand and grit out of my eyes.

"You can do this!" I repeated to myself. "Remember what

Mershnin said, you can fight, you can do this…"

At that point, the creature dropped to the ground and disappeared.

"What? Where is it?" I called out to Riola.

My hands trembled as I clutched the hilt of my blade, and my knees felt like jelly.

"Don't know," she replied, her eyes scanning the ground intently. "I heard stories about these on the mines—they're called Goyrin. Odd thing is, I thought they were only supposed to live in Gor…"

Wissh.

Crack!

The long, spiny tail flicked out of the sand. In one mighty stroke, it connected with Riola and the three trolls. I heard her shriek in pain, but before I could respond, a deafening screech shot through my ears, followed by a dull thud. Almost simultaneously, a great wash of sand flew into my face with such force that I spun around, falling face down in the sand. The Goyrin must have taken a swipe at me, too—luckily, it missed. With my eyes streaming and my face covered in dirt, I rolled over, wiped my brow with my sleeve, and readied my sword.

"Stand up! Stand up, silly," I told myself. "You're no good on the ground!"

I pulled myself onto my feet and saw the creature turn toward Riola. The Horbinn Cat darted about its feet in a rage, trying to get a grip with its claws. The Goyrin was almost impossible to tackle. Its translucent skin and spines were as hard as steel, and it changed color like a chameleon. One minute it was sandy brown and the next it was sky blue; my eyes got tired trying to follow it.

I was absolutely determined to do my best to protect Riola. The trolls had withstood the first blow. Riola, on the other hand, had been knocked several feet, landing in a heap on the ground. I chased the beast through the deep, hot sand for all I was worth. Just before it reached her, I lunged as hard as I could, piercing one of its legs. The Goyrin turned pitch black, let out a hiss, and swung around to face me.

With another ear-splitting screech, it directed the next sweep of its tail right at me.

Whip!

Crack!

I leapt through the air, narrowly avoiding the strike. Braced for a third attack, I discovered that the horrid creature wasn't interested in me. Quick as a flash, it turned its attention back to Riola, attempting to pounce on her crumpled body. I threw myself forward as fast as I could and lashed out again, this time at its tail. As I brought my sword down, something inside me whispered, "Don't slice, stab between the spines."

"That's it!" I exclaimed. With all my might, I plunged the point of my sword into the creature's flesh. To my surprise, it sank deep. Once again distracted, the Goyrin swung around to face me.

The Horbinn Cat had gotten a grip on one of the creature's wings and was attempting to tear it to pieces. But even the pale webbing between the wing bones was resilient.

"The cat and I aren't enough," I thought aloud. "Where are the trolls? The trolls must help us!"

Humphrey, Bella and Mrs. P made towards the Goyrin as quickly as they were able. As they connected with it, I heard screeches, bellowing, clawing, and the crunching sound of tusks breaking through scales. Here and there, I managed to pierce the horrid creature. At one point, I even nicked off the end of its tail. It was more luck than anything else, but the foul brute certainly felt the pain. It let out an ear-piercing squeal and fought back harder than ever, whipping its tail and lunging with its formidable jaws. I knew that if I was ever sent sprawling, one nasty bite would finish off the job.

The Horbinn Cat leapt right onto the head of the Goyrin. It finally got a hold with its claws, biting and scratching with the tenacity of a Bull Terrier, nearly blinding the surprised beast. In vain it thrashed its head about, trying to free itself from the cat's formidable grip. The old sage had been right; the Horbinn Cat was a good ally in times of battle. But at that moment, we heard a loud, dull thud.

To my dismay, another Goyrin fell out of the air like a torpedo—it must have been hiding in the sand nearby. This one was even larger than the first. It lashed at Mrs. P and Bella with a mighty crack of its tail, sending them tumbling across the sand. Bound to his two friends, Humphrey could barely fight. The trolls had become sitting ducks. The Horbinn Cat immediately shot across to confront the new foe. Although he was tough, he was no match for this huge Goyrin, and we were utterly exhausted.

I miscalculated a swipe from the first Goyrin's tail and was hurled into the sand. With my feet painfully knocked out from under me, I summoned all of my courage, rolled over, and raised my sword. The hideous creature, virtually on top of me, pegged my arm to the ground with one giant talon. It tightened its grip, and my sword dropped out of my hand.

In that moment of despair, something rose up from deep within me. I refused to accept death. The words of Mershnin sprang into my mind, "*If you are ever at your wits' end, do not accept defeat—call on Father Bruëll.*" For a split second, I saw the old man's kind, wise face smiling down on me. I found myself yelling out, for all I was worth, "Help us, Father Bruëll! Please help us!"

The Goyrin, about to bite my torso, released its grip and froze. The air went strangely quiet. I looked in the direction of the other horrid creature; it had also stopped in its tracks. Both of them cowered, their bodies changing to the exact color of the sand. They grimaced and hissed, fixing their eyes firmly on the sky above. Then, through the silence, a strange noise pealed out overhead, almost like the tearing of paper, but much louder. A bright, white light poured over us, gentle at first, then stronger and stronger every second. Finally, a loud noise rang out, like the thundering of a great wave crashing against a rock.

I looked up. My heart came close to bursting with wild, terrified excitement.

Two formidable creatures shot out of the sky. Were they winged horses? Perhaps. Each had the head of some sort of fierce animal, with flared nostrils, wide eyes, and loud snorting, but they were too bright, too majestic to look at. Each creature bore a magnificent rider carrying an enormous sword. Energy and life poured out of them. In their powerful presence, I felt no bigger than a mouse.

Within a few seconds, they had descended to about fifty feet above us. They paused, gathering energy. The Goyrin attempted to hide in the sand, but the glorious creatures swooped straight down towards them. Trapped, the Goyrin leapt into the sky in a desperate, and futile, attempt to escape. The two riders shouted a command, and their fiery creatures pounced, descending upon them in one final leap.

In the sky above, a furious battle raged. With swords glinting white and hot, a series of decisive blows sent the Goyrin reeling. One, fatally injured, tumbled out of the sky and landed with a thud a few hundred feet away.

At that point, the remaining Goyrin let out an awful screech, forcing me to block my ears. Four or five more arrived, snarling and hissing as they flew through the air. How cumbersome and slow they appeared in comparison to the glorious winged creatures! The watchful riders didn't miss a beat. One placed a horn to his lips and blew a long, clear note. The heavens tore open once again, and more of the glorious creatures arrived, each with a majestic rider. They descended so quickly that I could barely track them.

The Goyrin whirled about in the sky like maddened dogs, screeching and lashing out as they tried to fight. At each turn, the heavenly creatures easily outwitted them; their strength, beauty, and agility proved too much for the writhing, hate-filled beasts.

Just when we thought we'd been forgotten, the largest of the Goyrin caught sight of Riola. Changing from black to a glassy, translucent color, it dropped down for the kill. Without wasting a split second, one of the bright creatures tore after it, gripped the filthy lizard with its giant feet, and flung it across the desert sands. A few seconds later, a loud crunching sound rang out and another of the Goyrin tumbled into the Misran. The remaining creatures fled, desperate to save their lives.

And so the fighting ended almost as quickly as it began. The air became calm and peaceful, and the magnificent riders disappeared. The whole event had overwhelmed me. I sat speechless for a very long time. I relived the fantastic rescue—and my closest call with death. I felt exhausted, terrified, excited, and bewildered all at the same time.

Eventually, I hauled myself onto my feet and hobbled over to Riola and the trolls. They were also in a state of shock. Humphrey sat perfectly motionless, staring into the sky. The poor creature would've died if not for the white riders. Nasty gashes and long, painful streaks covered his body. Riola, Bella, and Mrs. P sat huddled together, bewildered and very sore, but alive.

The only one not silent or in shock was the Horbinn Cat. The curious animal paced back and forth, staring into the sky and leaping upward from time to time.

"I think he wants to join the riders," croaked Riola. "That animal is either wildly courageous, or completely insane."

"At least one thing is clear," she continued, "Father Bruëll definitely exists!"

"Yes, he does," I replied with a smile, "and he's on our side."

"How are you feeling?" I asked after a pause.

"Not too good, Cole, not too good at all. I can't walk. That first Goyrin sent me flying. It completely knocked the breath out of me, and bruised my ribs. I twisted my ankle when I landed—the same foot that the Myurim injured. I won't be much use for a while."

"And you have a few really nasty cuts, too," I said, looking at her wounds. "You'll need some serious bandaging."

"There's some clean cloth in one of the bags," she replied, "and a new bottle of ointment that I bought from the market. I can dress my own wounds, but you'll need to help the trolls."

I made my way over to the bags, which lay scattered across the sand, and rummaged through them. Once I had found the cloth and ointment for Riola, I cleaned the wounds of each troll. Although badly hurt, the resilient creatures seemed in good spirits. Each had put up a courageous fight and had survived against the odds.

Even Mrs. P, who had suffered the most, livened up when I spoke to her. When I finished dressing their wounds, I took a look at my own. I had acquired quite a collection since the journey began. I had cuts and scratches all over, as well as countless peck wounds from the crows, and a large imprint on my right arm, a horrid reminder of the Goyrin's talons.

It was late afternoon by then, and the sun's rays were steadily disappearing. I looked into the distance and saw how close we'd come to the mountains—we were perhaps an hour's walk away.

"We need to get there," I said with determination. "Right into Father Bruëll's territory. While we're still here, in the land of Lord Grimmon, we'll never be completely safe."

"OK," replied Riola wearily, "but I can't walk."

"You'll have to ride on one of the trolls," I answered. "Humphrey will manage, it isn't very far now."

Before anything else, however, we quenched our thirst and ate some of the food that Mershnin had given us. Once we had packed everything up, I helped Riola onto Humphrey's back, being careful to avoid his wounds. We walked slowly on the final leg of the journey; we were completely exhausted and in a lot of pain. Yet somehow, knowing that Father Bruëll did exist gave us the perseverance we needed. Things had finally begun to change, and the journey was worth the struggle.

As we pushed on, Riola and I began to talk about the crow and how it had been chanting in her ears. Lord Grimmon had obviously been trying to break her down ever since she escaped from the mines. Even without the walls, nasty guards, and hard labor, her soul remained imprisoned. The attack had been cunning; he'd used quiet whispers in her sleep, nothing more. How could she possibly have detected them? And, until they were detected, these voices were ceaseless. The attack must have worn her down more than we realized. Could I have been attacked like that, too?

I remembered the weird Nagara, who whispered his nasty message into my ear. I also thought about the peculiar sentry I'd met, who poured scorn on our journey and mocked Riola. I'd bet

Lord Grimmon had sent him. If I had believed him, if I had given in and gone my own way, none of us would have made it.

As I had guessed, we reached the mountains in less than an hour. What a sight they were! The magnificent range of smooth, purple-blue rocks extended from east to west, forming a barrier against all that was dark, cunning, and evil. As we got closer, the desert sands gave way to hard soil and rock. Small thorny bushes and shrubs dotted the landscape, and even a few little trees grew here and there. We came to a halt at the foot of the largest mountain, the very one that we had been aiming for.

"We've made it!" cried Riola. "We've actually made it!"

She slid off Humphrey, flopped onto the ground, and burst into tears.

"I didn't think we'd live to see this," she spluttered. "Do you know how long I've dreamed of this?"

The trolls collapsed beside her, huffing and puffing like small locomotives. And for a while, perhaps an hour or two, we sat there in silence, listening to the wind and regaining our strength.

"Are we safe here, or do we start climbing?" I finally asked.

"We need to climb," replied Riola. "I think these southern slopes are really no-man's-land, and I'm not spending the night out here. Father Bruëll's kingdom starts on the other side, once you reach the summit."

"Darn," I muttered aloud, "that's a real pain. Where do we begin? We can't simply climb anywhere; we might get stuck on a slope that's too steep for the trolls. We need to search for a safe route."

Riola looked about and noticed the start of a shallow gorge a hundred or so yards away.

"I think there could be a way up over there," she said, pointing out the direction. "Maybe you should go and check it out?"

"Good idea! I'll head over with the Horbinn Cat; you stay here with the trolls. If it's the most obvious route out of the Misran, we might meet some opposition."

Chapter Fourteen:

Into the Beautiful Realm

═══○○○═══

With the Horbinn Cat by my side, I mustered my courage and quietly crept towards the gorge. As I came closer, I realized the opening lay in a small alcove. Solemn statues, one of a man, the other of a woman, stood on either side. Beyond that, a few stairs led up to a path. It really seemed the only safe way; the mountains to the left and right were far too steep for the trolls. Then I thought: what if the stairs were designed to lure us into danger? I stood there for a while, wondering if I was about to walk into a trap.

"Would Lord Grimmon bother with that?" I wondered. "He knows that we'd call Father Bruëll."

I couldn't make up my mind. I needed guidance. We weren't clear of danger until we had reached the other side.

All of a sudden, the Horbinn Cat cocked his head to one side and pricked up his ears. He didn't act frightened or aggressive, but more curious than anything else.

"What have you seen?" I whispered.

A chill went down my spine. I felt something very strange in the air. I looked about cautiously, seeing nothing unusual. Yet, the feeling grew stronger; the hairs on the back of my neck rose. Slowly and quietly, I drew my sword. Then I glimpsed an enormous woman in the path ahead. Though her image appeared faint, her presence felt strong and beautiful. Looking at her peaceful and welcoming face, nothing in me felt threatened. Was she an angel? As quickly as she had arrived, she began to fade away. Before she disappeared entirely, I heard her say,

"*Forge ahead, Cole, forge ahead!*"

What a relief! That was more than the guidance I had hoped for. I returned to Riola and the trolls, and tried to explain what had happened.

"Sure, Cole," she said, "I'll go. It sounds safe. Help me back onto Humphrey, and let's get going."

She sounded more trusting than ever before.

So we made our way between the statues, up the steps, and into the rocky gorge that ascended the mountain. Rather than marching us right up to the highest peak, this route took us slightly to the left and towards one of the lower summits. The walk was neither easy nor overly tiring. We didn't have a care in the world; our spirits soared. We felt like we could've conquered anything. As if to make things easier, starting about halfway up, the pathway had been cobbled. Here and there, we even came across a few stairs that had been chiseled into the rock. Compared to the desert sands, this was a well-kept highway!

We stopped from time to time to enjoy the view, to rest, and to quench our thirst. With the threat of danger fading, only the steady approach of evening compelled us to push on. We reached the summit about an hour and a half later. There, the cobbled path widened out into a road, cutting its way through the top of the mountain. While we passed through, the road made a sharp turn, which led us out onto the other side of the range. We had finally entered the kingdom of Father Bruëll, and everything was different.

A deep, lush valley swept out before us. In the distance, another magnificent range of mountains basked in the evening light. The valley, mainly forested, had a number of glistening lakes that trailed in and out between the vegetation. The colors looked unbelievably crisp and vivid, almost as though an artist had painted the scene for us. The green of the plants was vibrant and bold, and the sky was on fire with metallic blues, reds, and yellows. The cool, humid air, sweet to breathe, was full of the aroma of wildflowers, as well as the rich, subtle smells of earth, moss, and herbs. Like a background symphony, the beautiful calls of little songbirds filled the air and, in the distance, we could hear the mysterious cries of unseen animals. Life surrounded us. In crossing the summit, we had surely crossed into another world.

The trolls instinctively stopped to rest, so Riola pushed herself off Humphrey's back and sat down beside him.

"So this is it," she said with a huge smile. "This is the land of Father Bruëll."

"It must be," I replied, flopping onto the ground. "And look at it. What a place!"

We both sat there for a while, taking in all the sights and sounds of this enchanted, beautiful realm. Somehow, my body knew that the day's journey had come to an end. Sure enough, I caught myself drifting off into dreamland. Standing up again, I shook my head and had a good stretch.

"Do you think we're going to have to travel all the way to those peaks?" I asked, looking over the valley.

"I don't really care," replied Riola. "We've made it, and now we're safe. Father Bruëll is somewhere here; it's simply a matter of time till we find him."

As I surveyed the range on the far side of the valley, something caught my eye. A tall, irregular shape rested at the base of one of the larger mountains. Straining my eyes a little, I could almost make out towers, parapets, and rows of carefully placed windows. If it was a building, it had been very cleverly designed, for it blended into the mountain almost perfectly. I wondered if part of it had been chiseled out of the rock face.

"Look over there, across the valley," I said to Riola. "Do you think that's a building, maybe a palace or something?"

"Wow!" she exclaimed, squinting into the distance. "You could be right. Perhaps we should head that way?"

"It'll be a job getting there," I replied. "Have you seen the road ahead?"

The narrow mountain pass wound down towards the valley in sharp, hairpin bends.

"We're going to need a lot of energy for that," I continued.

"Yes," interrupted Riola, "but we can face that tomorrow. Right now, we need somewhere to sleep. Why don't you see if you can find a cave or something?"

She was right; we did need somewhere to rest, and fast. The sun steadily dropped further and further behind the horizon. Once again, I went wandering off with the Horbinn Cat by my side. Luckily for us, we didn't have to search hard—we came across a small cave a few yards down the road. And what a find it was. A beautiful pattern had been engraved all around the edge of the entrance. I stared at the artwork for quite a while. The design definitely told a story; the figures and scenes had so much life they almost seemed to move.

"How did anyone do all of that with a chisel?" I wondered to myself. "It must have taken a lifetime."

The inside of the cave was clean, with a simple bench carved into the rock on each side—hard, but good enough to sleep on. The floor had enough space for the trolls. At the far end, two large, stone urns had been filled with water. I dipped my hand into one of them and cautiously took a sip; the water was cool and refreshing.

Perfect, I thought, this is all perfect.

That evening, we all bundled into the cave. We drank and washed as much as possible, had a meal, and then fell asleep. Although I kept the sword by my side, I knew in my heart that I wouldn't need it. We woke up late the next morning and discovered that a thick mist covered the whole area. It was difficult to see more than a few feet.

After breakfast, I helped Riola onto Humphrey's back. Then, when all was ready, we edged our way down the cobbled road and into the valley. A wall of stone, about two feet high, ran along the outer edge of the winding pass. It was good to know that it was there—it would've been easy to tumble down into the forest without it.

On our way down, I suspected that we were being followed. Whenever we stopped to rest, and the troll's chains no longer clinked or scraped, I heard a quiet pattering of paws or a rustle in the bushes that grew on the slopes. At one point, I dashed up onto a rock that jutted out from the mountainside. From there, I caught sight of a lone wolf. Probably about fifteen feet away, it would have been clearly visible if not for the mist. The beautiful animal stood watching me with its head slightly cocked to one side. I could see nothing menacing in its expression, only curiosity, so I called to it. The wolf edged forward a little, stared at me for a second or two, and then trotted off. I ran back to the road and caught up with the others.

Further and further we descended, winding our way through turn after turn in the road. The wolf continued to follow us, but always at a distance. As midday approached, the mist lifted, and the valley beneath opened up in all its splendor. I can't quite describe what it was like to be there, but there was more life and color than I could possibly take in.

The endless, playful chatter of the songbirds never ceased. Here and there, larger birds called to each other from hidden places. Bright little beetles crawled along the path at our feet and some took to the air, buzzing curiously about our faces. Every so often, we caught a glimpse of a massive eagle soaring high above. Down in the forest beneath, flocks of birds rose into the air and then disappeared again into the canopy.

How different this was from the Misran, or the Kkülm Trading Ruins. Riola and I, busy soaking it all in, hardly said a word to each other. After days of grueling travel, vicious battles, and narrow escapes, we almost found it hard to believe. This was especially true for Riola, who had been on the run long before I met her. She must have felt as though she walked in a dream. As for me, I wondered if I really wanted to go back to earth. This land made home look barren and confined. *Will Father Bruëll bring my parents here instead? Is that part of his plan?*

Eventually, the road brought us right down to the edge of a forest, where a breathtaking sight met us. An enormous angel stood in front of us, holding a gleaming sword. We stopped dead in our tracks—even the Horbinn Cat stayed absolutely still. And then it dawned on me that there was something familiar about this being. She had spoken to me the day before. This time, she appeared in all her glory, and her presence was so bright and powerful that I could almost feel it pushing me over.

"My name is Lythwellen," she announced, "and I will take you to Father Bruëll's house."

Then the most peculiar thing happened. She raised one hand and said in a clear, strong voice, "Into the water!"

At first, Riola and I were a little confused. Then we realized that Lythwellen was looking at something behind us. We turned around and, to our horror, we saw one of the Myurim. With our attention completely captivated by Lythwellen, we hadn't noticed the creature's approach. We didn't expect to see such a tormented beast in that peaceful place! Surprisingly, the Myurim showed no interest in attacking. It looked as if it was pleading.

"Into the water!" commanded Lythwellen again. This time, her voice had a piercing edge to it. I felt a short, sharp tremor pass through my body. The Myurim let out a groan, tore past us, and headed straight for a sparkling pool that lay several yards beyond. When it collided with the water, it let out a deafening cry. Then, almost as quickly, it fell asleep. Only its eyes and snout protruded above the surface.

"What is that doing here?" I asked in shock.

"You're not the only ones looking for freedom," replied Lythwellen. "He had been waiting his turn for a long time."

"What? Why would any of them want to be near Father Bruëll? Aren't they supposed to be evil to the core?"

"Yes, Cole, most of them are completely evil, and they were evil *before* they chose to become the Myurim. But a few were picked on and bullied until they agreed to join. They didn't have a clue what they were doing."

"So, did that one follow us here?" asked Riola in astonishment.

"Yes," replied Lythwellen, "and probably from when you were close to the end of the pass. It would've kept well behind you. The wretched creature didn't have the strength to enter the valley on his own; he was too fearful."

"That's strange," I said, "I didn't see anything follow us other than a lone wolf. Surely we would've noticed the Myurim's smell?"

"That would normally have been true," answered Lythwellen. "In the case of this one, however, the healing process began when he first chose to seek Father Bruëll's help. His journey has been a perilous one. When he arrived at these mountains, he wandered about in agony for many years, trying to raise the courage to face his fears and enter the valley."

"What a horrible life," I pondered aloud. "I suppose he's lucky to be here. How long will he stay asleep?"

"That's hard to tell," replied Lythwellen, "but I would imagine it'll be quite a while. I do know that, when he wakes up, he'll be the troll he was always meant to be."

"So…does Father Bruëll know he's here?" asked Riola.

"Of course he does," replied the angel, "and it was Father Bruëll who allowed him to cross over from the Misran. When he was an ordinary troll, his name was Mindinn, and perhaps one day you will meet him."

She turned her attention to the Horbinn Cat. "You have my leave, dear friend. You played your role with valor, as you always do, and now you are free to go."

The mysterious cat purred loudly in reply, and then disappeared into the trees.

"Come," said Lythwellen, "we must be on our way."

She guided us along a narrow path that wound its way deep through the heart of the forest. Over time, we became accustomed to the brightness and intensity of her presence. The serene and restful forest, on the other hand, made a part of me want to lie down and sleep. The trees had slender, tall trunks, reaching up high into the deep blue sky above. And the great, gleaming pools of water between them made everything shimmer with reflected light. More butterflies than I could count filled the air, many of them with striking colors and intricate patterns.

At one point, I heard a quiet but definite humming noise. I turned around to see a group of small lizard creatures with wings. From head to tail, they were striped in gold and bronze bands, and they hovered about like energetic hummingbirds—I imagine their eyes were on the insects, not the flowers.

In the shadows around the pools, bright little frogs croaked and creaked to each other. They hid when anyone got too near, making it almost impossible to see them up close.

Above all, I'll never forget the strange silence of that forest. Neither the colors nor the sounds of foraging animals could break the stillness and peace that rested on us. It felt as if every one of those great trees was in a deep, heavy sleep.

"Hush!" said Lythwellen at one point. "Stop for a moment and listen; listen very carefully."

Obediently, we kept absolutely still and tried to work out what she was talking about. And then, quite distinctly, we heard a rustling in the trees, followed by the rhythmic sound of large feet stepping methodically on moist ground.

A small herd of elephants broke across the path before us. For their size, they were masters of disguise and quietness. And what peculiar creatures they were! I had seen enough elephants in books to know that these were clearly of a different world. Extremely tall and graceful, each had two sets of long tusks; one set protruding upwards from above the eyes, and the other downwards from each side of the mouth. Their deep blue-green color blended perfectly with the foliage. They stepped carefully and deliberately, almost as if they were walking on a tightrope.

One departed from the herd, cautiously approached Riola, and sniffed about her face with the end of its long, probing trunk. It looked at her with its enormous dark eyes and a deep rumbling sound echoed out from its chest. Then, almost as quickly as it had arrived, the curious creature rejoined the heard. They set off again on their journey through the forest.

Lythwellen looked at me with a smile—she must have noticed my astonishment.

"You may recognize many of the animals here," she said. "And, yes, they will all be a little different from what you are used to."

She turned to the trolls.

"You faithful creatures," she exclaimed, "perhaps you would prefer to wade through the pools?"

Being parched and hungry, the trolls took up the invitation to revel in the soothing, cool ponds. Here and there, they would stop to feed on a root, a tuber, or a tantalizing water plant. Because of her injured ankle, Riola stayed on Humphrey's back the entire time. She got soaked through, and it didn't bother her in the slightest. Our bags also got drenched, but no one worried about that, either. Besides, delicious fruit covered many of the trees—we weren't exactly going to starve without our stale bread and cured meats.

"Lythwellen, do you know about our battle against the Goyrin?" I asked later in the day.

"I do," she replied.

"I've been wondering about a few things," I continued. "If Mershnin knew that we would face such a fierce attack, how did he expect me to do anything? Why did he even train me, or let us carry on with the journey alone? He must have known that we would need rescuing. Is that what he had in mind? It feels like he pretty much wasted a lot of time on me."

"No, he wasn't wasting his time when he trained you," replied Lythwellen. "He wouldn't have done it if he thought so. You had an important role to play, and he realized that."

"I wasn't any good!" I exclaimed. "I had so much confidence after Mershnin, but in the end, I didn't make a difference."

Lythwellen stopped and turned to face me. "Didn't make a difference?" she queried. "Are you sure about that?"

"Well…right now, I feel like a bit of a nobody. Yesterday I was nearly eaten alive and Riola was badly injured. I wasn't exactly the right person for the job."

Lythwellen bent down and looked me straight in the eyes. "You're not a nobody, Cole. Mershnin saw who you are. He saw in you a person that you do not yet know. He saw a fighter. He saw someone who is brave. He didn't see a nobody."

"I still don't think I made much of a difference," I complained. "They would've been better off with Mirrakin."

"You made a huge difference," replied Lythwellen. "Wasn't it you who noticed the evil crow whispering lies to Riola? And who, without weapon or training, bravely challenged that crow in a cave? You also endured the lies of the Nagara, and the wicked sentry. You stood up to one of the Goyrin and, against all odds, you prevented Riola from being murdered. Then, when things took a turn for the worst, you refused to surrender. You remembered Mershnin's words and you called on Father Bruëll. If not for your courage and determination, Riola and the trolls might well have died in the Misran. You walked into that battle a boy and, although you may not realize it, you walked out closer to being a man. Mershnin knew exactly what he was doing when he trained you."

"Trying to face life alone," she continued, "comes from pride and fear, not strength or wisdom. A single person could never have defeated the enemies you faced. Life is not supposed to work like that; victory was made to be shared."

"Lythwellen, why does Mirrakin like doing things alone?"

"His journey has not been an easy one, Cole, and now he fears too much to ask for help. He has convinced himself that he does not need it and, while he lives under that spell, he will be unable to see the truth – he has chosen to stay blind. Nonetheless, that is his story, so I'll leave him to tell you about it when the time is right."

"Oh…does that mean I'll meet him again?"

"Perhaps. Come; right now we need to keep moving. All your questions will be answered in good time."

CHAPTER FIFTEEN:

The River of Truth

══○○○══

We reached the other side of the forest by late afternoon. As the path broke through the last line of trees, we saw that the mountains were a short distance away. Right before us, however, we saw the gentle bank of a small, winding river.

Beyond the river lay a narrow stretch of forest, and from then onward the mountains rose higher and higher into the sky. The palace, which rested on the lower slopes, was almost in full view—only a few treetops blurred its shape. I had been right when I first saw that building, it was strange indeed. Parts of it had been hewn out of the rock face, and other areas were built of stone and wood. All in all, it blended into the environment so perfectly that it looked more like a living organism than a regular building. It trailed up the side of the mountain to quite a height, with splendid parapets rising here and there, gracious balconies dotted about, and elegant staircases spiraling upward from one point to another.

"Let's stop for a bit," said Lythwellen as we reached the river. "I think you know that this is no ordinary land, but when we cross that river, things will become even more different."

"Ah…how do you mean?" asked Riola.

"Well," replied the angel, "once we are on the other side of the bank, your eyes will change; you will see what a person really thinks of themselves, deep down inside. You will see their soul."

Riola dropped her head; she looked very pensive.

"I think I knew this would happen," she said quietly. "You can't have anything to hide here. You have to be who you really are: no secrets, no lies, no horrible pride."

"Exactly!" exclaimed Lythwellen. "Are you absolutely sure that's what you want?"

Riola thought for a while. She had dreamed of this moment for ages, of finally being in Father Bruëll's land. Now that she had arrived, it was in some ways a little scary.

"Yes," she finally said, "I will cross the river. I'm not turning back now."

"And you?" inquired Lythwellen, looking me in the eyes. "What have you decided?"

"Ah…well," I responded, "I'm not staying alone on this side of the bank."

In truth, I don't think I understood why Riola was so anxious.

"Then it is settled," declared Lythwellen. "We shall swim across the river."

"Huh, swim across?" I queried. "Where's the bridge?"

"Not this time," she answered with a smile. "Gabriel has other things to do right now; on this occasion you get to swim. It's fairly deep, but the current is gentle. There is nothing to fear. Each of us has to swim through. I'll help Riola off Humphrey's back and, if necessary, we can help her once she's in the water."

And so we entered the river, wading deeper and deeper until the ground beneath our feet disappeared and we were fully immersed. It was a short swim, and the trolls coped far better than I thought they would. When we climbed out on the opposite bank, things certainly were different.

Riola looked much younger, but not in a healthy way. Her body appeared thin and gaunt, her eyes large and dull, and her bones protruding. Her tattered clothes had become mere rags, and her hair sparse and straggly. She looked famished; I had to stop myself from gasping. Towards the end of the journey, Riola had been worn out, but now she looked absolutely shocking.

Lythwellen reached out and gave her a warm, reassuring hug.

"You have nothing to prove here," she said quietly, "nothing at all. And there is no shame either, only the promise of wholeness."

"What…what just happened?" I stuttered.

"Remember what I said," answered the angel. "You are seeing her soul, Riola the way she sees herself. Right now, she doesn't believe she's worth very much, but that will soon change."

"Oh," I replied quietly, a little stunned at what we'd agreed to.

Riola was silent.

I gazed down at my own body, and then at my feet, legs, and hands.

"What?" I spluttered aloud. "I'm—I'm so young…a small boy!"

I looked up at Lythwellen in utter disbelief. She seemed bigger and brighter than ever, like a beautiful giant towering over me.

"Don't be alarmed," she replied. "You're older now than you were a few days ago, though I know you may struggle to believe that. Right now, who you really are and how you see yourself are two different things. Your soul will grow and mature as each day passes, and you will learn to accept yourself."

Strangely enough, the trolls didn't look too different. Lythwellen explained that they had no ability to lie or to see themselves as other than they really were. She also spoke of the damage they'd suffered in the mines, and how they needed a lot of healing.

After leaving the river, we helped Riola back onto Humphrey. We walked into the small strip of forest that grew at the foot of the mountains. The air felt heavier with each step we took. I know that sounds strange; I always struggle to describe it. Imagine air that you almost have to drink, rather than breathe.

The colors of the plants and trees were even more rich and vivid than in the valley. Above us, the sunlight glowed warm bronze.

We left the forest and made our way up towards the palace walls.

"Finally, our destination!" exclaimed Lythwellen with a warm smile. "Well done to you all, you have been courageous travelers!"

As we got closer, I noticed a detachment of knights standing guard at the gates. They were tall and solid, and covered from head to foot in gleaming armor. One of them stepped forward and called out in a loud voice.

"They have arrived!"

The enormous gates swung open. Two knights broke off and escorted us into the palace grounds. We went up a magnificent avenue that wound its way between ancient, glorious trees, right to the foot of the palace doors. Knights stood all along that avenue, each as muscular and vigilant as the next. Scattered beneath the garden trees, we saw bustling groups of people, who must have been from every culture under the sun. And not just people—I caught sight of angels larger and more awesome than Lythwellen. Some were tall and solemn, while others were fiery and fierce.

When we reached the palace doors, attendants greeted us. They spoke with Lythwellen for a few minutes, then led us through the entrance. They took us to have our wounds cleaned and carefully dressed. Talitha, one of the younger staff members, offered to stay by Riola's side and to support her when she walked. While they tended to us, others unloaded our baggage, and then led the three trolls to a place where they could rest.

Compared to the bustling activity of the gardens, the palace was cool and quiet. When we were ready, Lythwellen led us down a central hallway, through a grand arch, and past a number of warm alcoves and colorful rooms. I saw tiled reception areas decorated with beautiful, intricate patterns. I also remember spacious lounges that had thick, lush carpets and graceful curtains. Here and there, a sweeping staircase led up to another floor. While the palace looked large from the outside, it seemed absolutely huge once we were inside.

We were given our own rooms on the ground floor, which made things a lot easier for Riola; she didn't have to climb any stairs. Each room had a large window looking out onto the forest, its own bathroom, and closets filled with clothes, towels, and soaps. We had a few hours to rest, bath, and get changed before the evening meal. It felt wonderful to finally climb out of our filthy rags and put on some decent clothes.

Talitha collected us for dinner, leading us to an enormous dining room. In the center, a single, sturdy table ran from one end to the other. A mass of people sat around it. I hadn't expected it to be so informal; groups came and went throughout the evening. Some huddled together in quiet dialogue; others were loud and jovial. Great bowls of fruit, cuts of meat, glasses of wine, and pitchers of water were passed up and down throughout the night. It was all laughter, chatter, and the constant clattering of cutlery and crockery. Riola and I felt a little overwhelmed by it all. Considering how we looked since crossing the river, we decided to sit at the far end of the table. As soon as we were settled, Talitha left us to enjoy the evening.

We ate to our heart's content. Then a talkative character came and sat to my left. Short and stocky, he had bright little eyes and a broad smile.

"*Glimmin ru winden?*"

"Cole, I think he's trying to talk to you," whispered Riola.

"*Glimmin ru winden?*"

She was right; the curious individual was trying to ask me something, but I had no idea what he was saying.

"Sorry, I can't understand you," I replied, trying to talk as clearly as I could over all the noise.

"*Ah! Yimoryn al enor!*"

Once again, I tried to explain that his words made no sense to me, but he was completely unbothered. With a loud laugh, he slapped me on the back and chatted away with rising enthusiasm. This carried on for quite a while, and I started to think that I had made a new friend. Riola smiled her way through the whole episode. She probably found it quite funny, and I think she was also glad that she hadn't got caught up in the confusion. When we finished eating, Talitha arrived to see how we were doing. She took one look at our tired eyes and led us back to our rooms. That night we slumped into bed like felled trees!

The following morning we woke up late. As soon as we got out of bed, Talitha appeared, offering to help Riola. When we were changed and ready, we made our way to breakfast. Things were lively and chaotic, like dinner the night before, so we returned to our quiet spot and watched the endless bustle and chatter. On our long trek through Khülm, we had grown used to our own company. Besides that, Riola wasn't familiar with so much laughter and happiness. Looking back on it all, she must have felt very self-conscious, sitting at such a wonderful banquet in her thin, disheveled body. But no one even looked twice—they must have been used to the arrival of needy refugees.

When we had finished eating, Talitha returned and told us that Riola would spend the day resting, while I helped wash the trolls. One of the attendants led me out of the dining room, into the kitchen, through a back door, then across a paved courtyard and into some stables on the opposite side. They were built around a quadrangle, with a sunken area in the center used for washing and grooming. Right there in the middle, Humphrey, Bella, and Mrs. P sat patiently. Before the attendant went back to his duties, he asked me to stay there and wait for the groomsman.

Although it felt good to see the trolls again, I did feel a little lost waiting around for the groomsman; he took ages to arrive. Eventually, I heard the sound of a familiar voice.

"*Ah! Yimoryn al enor!*"

I turned around and saw the curious little fellow from the night before. He walked right up to me with a beaming smile and slapped me on the back.

"Nomin et Byor! Byor!" he exclaimed repeatedly, pointing at his chest.

"Ah, right," I thought, "your name is Byor!"

We were doing a lot better than we had the first time around. I hadn't picked up on his name the night before. I called him Byor from then on, but every time I said it, a quirky smile came over his face. I probably didn't pronounce it right. He struggled with my name just as much; the best he could manage was *Chorl*. Despite this, language never seemed to bother Byor. He was as talkative as ever that morning. Luckily for me, he used his hands more than his mouth when he spoke, which made him a little easier to understand.

First, we thoroughly soaked the trolls with buckets of water, then we gave them a good scrub. After that, we cleaned their hooves, examined and polished their tusks, inspected their eyes, and checked their ears for parasites. Byor was very good with animals, and perhaps more of a vet than a groomsman. He had a large briefcase with him, with all sorts of instruments and medicines. He made Mrs. P swallow some potion, which she obediently did. It couldn't have tasted very nice; it made her squirm.

After lunch, the attendant returned and asked me to join Riola in the gardens.

I finally found her sitting with Talitha on the brow of a small hill that overlooked a vineyard. The two of them had been there for most of the morning, resting under the shade of a tree and talking to those who passed by. They invited me to join them, so we enjoyed the view together for a while, chatting about all that had happened.

The sun began to set and a cool breeze carried with it the rich fragrance of wild flowers. Birds chirped in the garden, with the constant drone of bees searching for pollen in the background. And then, quite unexpectedly, we became aware of someone else's presence. We looked up. A man approached, dressed in a richly woven robe. His eyes were bright and lively, and his expression was welcoming.

"Hello, Riola; hello, Cole," he said with a warm smile. "My name is Abbanyll, and I'll be taking you to Father Bruëll. He would like to meet the two of you."

He led us back through the gardens and towards the palace.

CHAPTER SIXTEEN:

The King and the Splendid City
═○○○═

My heart pounded and my palms felt clammy. We had come to the end of our journey, and I was going to meet the Father, the King of the land. This was why we had been travelling for days on end—for Riola it had been months. We had endured being spied on, chased, imprisoned, and attacked. The moment of truth had arrived, and I felt unprepared. I had cleaned up as much as I could after helping with the trolls, but I still felt ragged and a bit smelly. Besides that, I had never met royalty before. What was I supposed to say? More importantly, what wasn't I supposed to say?

"Riola," I whispered, "what should I do when we meet Father Brüell?"

"Don't *do* anything," she replied. "There's no fooling anyone here. Just be yourself."

Abbanyll led us through the palace, like when we had first arrived. This time, however, Humphrey, Bella, and Mrs. P came with us. A number of attendants joined in to help move their chain and to prevent pieces of furniture from being knocked over. Thankfully, we never went up any of the spiral staircases.

After passing through a few lounges, halls, and meeting areas, we went through an arched, double doorway and into a large courtyard paved with flagstones. The palace wall overlooking the courtyard had the most beautiful paned windows. Three high walls surrounded the other sides of the yard, making it feel safe and protected. The most enormous fig tree that I had ever seen grew in the center. Rising out of a knot of massive roots, its trunk split and split again into twirling, twisted branches that unwound into the sky. Rich with fruit, it filled the area with a sweet fragrance.

A large number of people bustled about. Dignitaries from

foreign lands, attendants, and plenty of ordinary folk, stood about deep in conversation, or hurried on, busy with some task. Abbanyll led us through the court and towards the fig tree. Before we reached the center of the crowd, he kindly asked us to wait where we were for a minute or two, while he went further. Talitha excused herself and returned to the palace.

We waited for a few minutes, with the bewildered trolls by our side, right in the thick of the colorful crowd. All of a sudden, as if by a signal we didn't know, the courtyard began to clear. The little groups of dignitaries and ordinary folk moved back into the palace. Soon a space opened up in front of us. For the first time, we caught a glimpse of someone sitting on a throne.

A man, dressed in a simple but beautiful garment, sat on a throne that looked as if it had been carefully sculpted from a single rock.

When we first met Lythwellen in the forest, I remembered how strength had poured out of her until I felt like it could have pushed me over. I felt the same with this man, but his presence was so much stronger. I knew that he was Father Bruëll.

In a strange way, I felt torn in two. One part of me was desperate to run and hide, while another part was so curious that it wouldn't let me go.

Very soon the courtyard was completely empty. Father Bruëll looked up from his throne; he was a king, for sure. What surprised me was how natural and relaxed he looked. I had expected someone distant and very formal, but he was nothing like that.

"Riola!" he called, rising to his feet. "You precious woman, you made it!"

He came over to us, threw his arms in the air with delight, and gave her an enormous hug. Dumbfounded, Riola had no idea how to respond.

"Come," he said, supporting her by the arm. "Come and talk with me."

The two of them walked back to the throne, where Abbanyll helped her climb up beside him.

Once they were seated and comfortable, Father Bruëll called

Humphrey, Bella, and Mrs P. His gentle voice carried an almost tangible weight and authority; the trolls didn't hesitate to respond. Then I felt a gentle touch on my shoulder, so I turned around. Lythwellen stood behind me. I had been so distracted that I hadn't even noticed her.

"Cole," she said in a quiet voice, "let's give them a little space."

We stepped back a few discreet paces.

I couldn't hear what they said, but I didn't need to. Riola went from looking unsure to smiling, and from smiling to laughing, and from laughing to a solemn expression. Then she burst into tears. And through the crying, I heard a few of Father Bruëll's words.

"Let them go, Riola. You don't need the trolls anymore."

"Don't they need me?" she asked. "I've been looking after them for so long now."

"Not anymore," he replied warmly. "You're here now and they are safe. You can let them go."

Riola flopped into his arms, her tears rolling down her cheeks and over his hands.

The trolls shuffled about nervously. Then, without warning, a great cracking sound pierced the air, followed by another, and then another. I turned to look at the trolls.

The links in their chain splintered. The shattering continued as Riola cried. The poor trolls froze with shock. In little more than a few minutes, and without any struggle, they had been set free from the shackles that had bound them for years.

"Weren't those chains made of iron?" I stammered aloud.

"Yes, they were," replied Lythwellen, "but it was Riola's fear that actually kept them there. After her father died, she was determined never to be alone again."

When she had stopped crying, Father Bruëll spoke again.

"Riola, this is your home now," he said. "This is your family, where you are loved."

She could hardly say a word. Once again, tears streamed down her face—this time from pure joy. When she stopped sobbing, Abbanyll wiped away her tears with his robe, took her by the hand,

and helped her down. Her foot had healed so she walked normally, but she probably didn't even realize it.

"We're not quite finished," said Abbanyll. "Will you let me take away the chains that bind you?"

"The chains that bind *me*?" she questioned. "I thought that only the trolls were bound."

"No, the trolls are not the only ones that are bound," he replied.

And with that, he uttered a commanding word or two in a loud voice.

Although I couldn't understand the language he used, something strange happened to my eyes. At first they itched, then they watered. Finally, a strong burning sensation passed over them. I couldn't see properly then, but when it ended, I saw Riola standing in front of the throne. Chains completely covered her whole body, which didn't seem to bother her in the slightest. She stood with her head tilted towards the sky, her eyes completely fixed on something. I lifted my head and almost fell over in surprise.

A magnificent city rose behind the palace and stretched up into the mountain above. It absolutely glowed with warmth and light. I stared in complete wonder and saw that both angels and people inhabited it. Each and every one, whether human or spirit, was completely unique; some were short and stocky, others tall and ethereal, some appeared loud and busy, while others were gracious and deliberate. A great number were dressed in fine, woven garments, while many more were clothed in color and light. I saw enormous warriors preparing for battle, skilled artists pouring color onto canvas, and clusters of musicians giving beautiful performances. People chatted and laughed in groups, or bustled from here to there. A regal flight of stairs led down from the city towards the palace. I could hardly take in the whole rich, vibrant scene.

"How in the world!" I exclaimed. "When did they all arrive?"

"They have always been here," answered Lythwellen. "You are now seeing things as they really are. It's quite a shock, isn't it?"

"I must have been completely blind," I spluttered. "But why didn't we see all of this—or even Riola's chains—after we crossed the river?"

"That would have been too much, too soon," replied Lythwellen. "I allowed you to see what you were ready to see at the time."

Our conversation ended and I turned my attention back to the throne.

"Riola," said Abbanyll a second time, "will you let me remove your chains?"

Riola pulled her eyes away from the splendid city, looked at him, and then down at her torso.

"What? What?" she stammered. "Where did these come from?"

"They've been there a long time," he replied. "Some wrapped themselves around you after your mum died, some clung to you when your father left, and even more latched onto you in the mine."

Riola paused, her eyes wide and startled as she ran her fingers over the links.

"Please take them away," she cried aloud. "I don't want to wear these horrid things!"

Abbanyll grasped them in his hands, shattering them one by one.

"Wow, that's no ordinary person," I whispered to Lythwellen. "Where does his strength come from?"

"You're right, Cole, he's no ordinary person at all. He is Father Bruell's son, powerful yet gentle. As you know, his name is Abbanyll, but some also call him Friend, or Brother. Those chains are no more than paper in his hands."

When he finished, Riola collapsed to the ground, sitting there for a while in silence. She looked at the remnants of the shackles that had bound her for years, shackles that had grown harder and harder with the passing of each day. I had often seen their effect in her eyes, the fear, worthlessness, anger, shame, and distrust. What a relief it must have been to be free from all of that!

For Riola, reality felt a little different and she began to look distressed. Abbanyll got down on his knees and put his arms around her.

"My beautiful sister," he said, "you may feel naked, because the chains no longer cover you, and you may feel weak, because they no longer hold you. Have courage! Now it is time for you to grow into the person you were made to be."

He helped her to her feet. Father Bruëll placed an exquisite gown over her, all woven in threads of purple, crimson, and gold.

"Oh, it's beautiful, but…but I could never wear this!" she exclaimed. "It's far too large, and I'm just—

Before she could finish her sentence, Father Bruëll swept her up, enveloping her in a huge embrace.

"No, keep it on," he encouraged. "You will grow into it; it was made for you."

When Father Bruëll finally released Riola from his enfolding arms, the girl who stood before us was a changed person. Her skin had the beginnings of a deep glow to it, her hands hung open rather than clenched, and she no longer looked gaunt and hunched with pain. She stood with dignity and delight. I stepped back, a little unsure of how to respond. I only knew how to talk to the old Riola—the Riola who cared, but was blunt, worn, and alone. Father Bruëll spoke first.

"Riola," he said with a smile, "I must talk a little with Cole. Will you let Lythwellen take you inside?"

Riola lifted her head and, beaming from ear to ear, she threw her hands in the air and shouted aloud, "Thank you, thank you so much!" She literally bounded over to Lythwellen, and together they made their way back across the courtyard and into the palace.

The trolls stayed huddled together, bewildered by what had happened. Then they saw a friendly face in the courtyard; it was Byor, accompanied by three attendants.

"Humphrey!" he called out. "*Yun ta'vor,* Humphrey!"

The old troll stood pondering for a while, glancing between Byor and the chains that had bound him for so very long. And then, with a gentle snort, he shuffled off towards the lively groomsman. One of the attendants stepped forward, greeted Humphrey, and then led him across the yard and out through the doors. In the same way, Bella and Mrs. P were escorted from the court, one by one, and each with their own attendant. Once they had made their exit, Byor bowed and left, closing the doors behind him.

"Cole! Cole the courageous. I have looked forward to meeting you."

Father Bruëll's voice reassured me, but I still felt a little scared. Summoning all of my strength and courage, I approached the throne. By the time I stood at his side, my heart was pounding and my palms were clammy. He looked directly into my eyes and held out a hand.

"Thank you," he said solemnly. "Thank you so much for protecting Riola. You did more than was asked of you, Cole, and I will always remember that. You could have tried to fight your way home by yourself, but you didn't. Yes, it was fear that determined your path in the beginning, but you went on to accept Mershnin's words of wisdom. You allowed the little courage you had to grow. Despite the many lies and obstacles that came against you, you accepted the invitation to play your part in a bigger story. Step by step you rose to the challenge. Now you are here and so is Riola."

Staring into his eyes, I completely forgot myself. I even forgot how small and young I felt; it all faded away. I have no idea how long that moment lasted.

Then my body felt stronger, and my soul was firm and peaceful. Even if no one else noticed the change, I knew with confidence what had happened inside me.

"Cole," he said after a pause, "I am going to return you, for now, to your parents, to your world."

His words sent my mind back to where it had all begun, to the incident with Shyla and the long journey from Aunt Anne's house.

"Yes," he continued, "your mum and dad are still alive, and they need you."

I breathed a deep sigh of relief. I would see them again; it would be safe to go home. Yet the more I thought about it, the more I wondered what it would be like to leave the magnificent land I was in. Did I really want to go back to the world of homework, pajamas and washing up duties? Father Bruëll must have known what I was thinking.

"Don't despair," he said reassuringly, "it won't all be the same when you return—you are a new person now. And remember, it doesn't end here; your journey has just begun."

"Thank you," I replied quietly. I wanted to say more, but I felt too overwhelmed to find the right words. A part of me wanted to stay there in the moment, to make it last as long as possible.

"What about Riola and the trolls?" I asked after a pause. "Will I see them again?"

"Yes," he answered, "you will see them before you leave tomorrow morning. Riola will stay here to heal and grow stronger for a long time. I won't send her anywhere soon, but you never know. In years to come, you may meet her again in this very palace."

Once our conversation had come to an end, Abbanyll approached the throne and took me by the hand, as he had done with Riola. He led me across the courtyard and back to the palace door, where Lythwellen waited for us.

"I look forward to seeing you again, Cole," he said. He gave me a warm embrace, then returned to the throne, where a retinue of angels had gathered around him and Father Bruëll.

Before the light became too intense, I saw the angels accompanying them up the staircase to the shining city. When my eyesight returned to normal, they were gone.

The air in the courtyard became still and quiet once again. The giant fig tree stood, as it always had, with its enormous branches reaching up to the moonlight. Lythwellen and I stayed there for a while, enjoying the silence. And then, quite unexpectedly, it began to rain—a few drops at first, then a shower. We headed for the shelter of the palace. As soon as we entered the doors, the sky literally burst open, releasing a torrent of water.

Lythwellen walked me back through the palace to the dining area.

"There is someone who would like to chat with you," she said. "I will leave you here and be on my way."

I glanced across the table and saw Riola seated at one end. She looked radiant, wearing an exquisite dress and her new robe. I walked over and pulled out the chair beside her.

"Hello," I said, "you look beautiful!"

"Thank you, Cole," she replied.

"Mind if I sit here?" I asked politely.

"Don't be silly," she answered, "of course you can!"

"Cole," she said a little later, "you are a true friend. I could never repay you for all that you have done for me. How do I thank you?"

"Well," I replied, "you showed me a whole new world, and you introduced me to Father Bruëll; I should be thanking you."

Riola smiled from ear to ear. She was free, and everything about her glowed.

And so we sat, chatting until we were the last ones at the table. Everything felt new and fresh. Like all good things, that evening ended, too. Eventually we grew tired and decided that it would be wise to go to bed. Neither of us knew what the future held, but we did know that it would be good.